Paradise Lost

~~

By Shiloh Callaghan

CIPHER
BOOKS

Foward

Introduction from the author

In the 17th century, twelve poetic books were compiled to form the masterfully written and acclaimed work "Paradise lost".

This is NOT that book.

Unlike Milton's work, in "Paradise Lost" by Shiloh Callaghan, the original sin has already occurred; the protagonist jailed; And those who survived the worlds apocalypse are now stranded on the remaining piece of earth that makes up their home.

Although the underlying theme of this tale is stitched together with the essence of the original "paradise lost", it greatly differs from Milton's approach and style of story telling.

This is a book of fantasy, science fiction and humor.
There is no Adam, Eve, Satan or the like. There are instead Atheist, Believers, Agnostics and Deceivers (which rhymes with believers).

I make no attempts to compare myself to the great English Poet. However I do feel strongly compelled to retell the biblical tale to an audience of our century's consciousness. Which is why YOU as the modern reader have also been given a roll to play in this "Dramody". Yes, YOU are a

Shiloh Callaghan

character in the story of "Paradise Lost", the tale that connects humanity's beginning to its End.

Paradise Lost

And I saw an angel coming down out of heaven with the key of the abyss and a great chain in his hand. And he seized the dragon, the original serpent, who is the Devil and Satan, and bound him for a thousand years. And he hurled him into the abyss and shut [it] and sealed [it] over him, that he might not mislead the nations anymore until the thousand years were ended. After these things he must be let loose for a little while.

Revelation 20:1-4

Shiloh Callaghan

Table of Content

Paradise Lost

Acts 1

First law: Create with Love

Shiloh Callaghan

ACT 1 SCENE 1: Introduction

"Can YOU see it? Yes, YOU. It's hard not to, its everywhere, It's everything. The word disaster is almost complementary. Wouldn't YOU agree?

It wasn't always like this you know. My home used to be a place of beauty and light. A place of miracles.

Now look at my hands, look at my mouth!

Before creation itself released from these fingertips, power dispersed from the tip of my very tongue. My dreams could become realities, my desires could come to fruition, I was a god, we all were.

But that was before the rebellion. Before Kaustos broke the divine law of our civilization.
And low and behold a war of Nightmares left all of this... ash in its wake.

In the end, it was decided by someone that we could no longer handle the power that had been bestowed upon us. And with one final creation came these... These cursed shackles of hands and of tongues!

Can YOU see that building behind me? It's the biggest one. Tall and ghostly looking isn't it? This is the prison that holds Kaustos. He has waited a longtime for YOU. And now that YOU are here, our story can continue. We can once again become free to create, free to dream and free ... to destroy!

Paradise Lost

Thank YOU.

For YOU are the final key that we needed to end...well, everything."

Shiloh Callaghan

ACT 1 SCENE 2: Lecture of love

"To create with love! Love I say, sweet love! The most powerful motivation in the universe! Oh I can almost feel it touching my insides! That is what our society was based on. We knew nothing else, only the purest of bla bla bla ba bla bla zzzzzz... We have a dreamer I see!" The professors voice rang out in Collin's ears as his elbow was yanked off the desk by the old man.

SMACK!

The boys sleeping head came crashing down.

"Ouch!" he cried as his noggin bounced from the table. Collins eyes opened to find his nutty looking Professor grinning down upon him.

"Tell us, did wonders fuse together on the canvas of your mind?!"

"What?" answered Collin, rather embarrassed.

"Dreams my boy! Did you have one?"

"No. None of us do sir."

The professor looked around the classroom. "ummm... yes, you all were born after the war. But no matter! I am confident that one day you all will dream! Maybe you will be the first Collin! I can see it now, panda's swimming in rainbows, blowing kisses to throngs of flowers below! Haha! Wouldn't that be an extraordinary first dream!"

The awkward silence that fallowed seemed to weigh down on the Professors smile and gesturing arms. Clearing his throat to speak in a more serious tone he continued his lecture,

"Love leads to inspiration. And even in a world lacking a muse, I believe love can create one. And why is finding a muse so important? Yes, you, the fat one." Professor Stone's finger pointed to the boy behind Collin.

"Because it's the first step to dreams and dreams can turn into creations."

"Exactly! We just need one person to be freed of these cursed shackles! Then we will be able to create once again! Won't that be exciting?!"

The professor waited for an overwhelming HARA! like he had experienced in previous years. Sadly apathy was the only taste placed in his mouth.

"Umm." He said in a moment of reflection. "That is, if you still believe in our ability? In our history?"

The professor walked towards the front of the class, mumbling gibberish to himself.

"What is he saying?!" Whispered the girl sitting next to Collin.

Shiloh Callaghan

"I don't know."

He rigorously began writing on the chalk board, jotting down these words:

Our mouth and our hands are covered, but our eyes are not! Paradise was a hoax!

"Yesterday I found this written on the bathroom wall. Now, whoever wrote it, is correct, partially anyway. Your eyes are not covered. And I am sure many, if not all of your eyes have read Professor Dante's scroll, 'Our hidden history from before the ash', Am I right?"

The students all nodded, now with a spark of interest.

"Okay, well my word seems to hold no weight when compared to the assumptions of a boy-man like Dante. So let's practice what he preaches. For tonight's homework, I want you all to visit The Tower. Maybe your eyes can teach you what my words no longer can. And tomorrow we will have a discussion about it in comparison with the young Professors theory. Class dismissed!"

Collin turned to his desk mate, "Did the bell already ring Willow?"

"Keep your voice down!" she scolded "lets go before he kills us all with boredom from another love lesson."

"I love to learn about... Love" spoke Philip, the fat kid that sat behind them.

Paradise Lost

"That's sweet" said Collin with a laugh, "So you guys want to visit The Tower and get our homework over with or what?"

"We could" Spoke Willow, "or since we all have seen it a thousand times before, we can skip it. Let's go somewhere else instead."

"Where do you have in mind?" asked Collin.

The girl's mouth-shackle* rose from a smile.

*A "mouth-shackle" is the metal plate with covers the mouths of all inhabitants. Along with the metal glove "hand-shackles", they both stop all from being able to create. Have a nice day!

Shiloh Callaghan

ACT 1 SCENE 3: The edge of the world

The three stood over the edge of their world and looked down into the dense fog below.

"What do you think is down there?" asked Philip.

"One way to find out" said Willow as she pretended to push her friend over the ledge.

"Ahhh!" The boys high pitch scream filled the air, echoing threw the fog. "Don't joke like that, Willow! Now I will have even worse nightmares!"

"Oh calm down" she huffed, "For a 16 year old, you scream like a baby girl!"

"Well, if you had nightmares as bad as mine, you would too!"

"Okay, enough" interjected Collin. "Willow's an idiot, Philip's a girl, lets all move on."

"Shut up Collin!" Both said with a bit of a laugh.

For the next hour or so they stared off of the edge, trying to spot any break in the haze. With wanting eyes they all hoped to catch a glimpse of what, if anything was down below. But like every other time before, they saw nothing.

The wind began to steadily pick up, forcing all three to step back slowly as the fog rolled in and blanketed their eyes.

Paradise Lost

"The wind is so strong!" said Philip.

Collin glanced over at his friend. Picking up a rock and threw it into the wind.

3,2,1

"Ouch!" yelled Philip as the breeze shot the rock back into the boy's leg.

"Be careful!" Said Willow with a serious tone "If that rock didn't blow back, it could have hit someone at the bottom!"

When the wind died down Collin gingerly responded to his friend, "It's been a longtime, Willow, you still believe there IS a bottom?"

"What, you still believe that there ISN'T one? Professor Dante was right, the world was never round, nothing broke away! Underneath this edge of fog may actually be something worth living for!"

"Don't be stupid, Willow!" Said Philip "Dante is full of rubbish, isn't that right Collin?"

Collins eyes looked over at the real reason why they came here. It was where Willow would visit everyday after school; today was no exception.

"If he is full of rubbish, it's what killed him."

The other two looked over as well. One of the few remaining trees left-standing after the war laid to the right,

Shiloh Callaghan

with its big roots clinging to the Cliffside. Its trunk and branches had been gnarled by a constant beating of the wind that blew from afar. The tree was old and ugly, but strong and stable.

One year, almost to the day, actually. That's how long it had been since Professor Dante and many others decided to attach the thick rope to one of the limbs that hung over the edge,

"'Adventure and beauty lies in the unknown, whereas lies and a constant dread have made up the known'… a lot of people believe those words" said Collin.

Willow stepped towards the tree. "Maybe that long rope wasn't such a crazy idea, they could have made it to the bottom. Maybe now they are finding all of the things that make up dreams." The girl had a longing as she spoke.

"It could be, Willow" responded Collin, "but that would mean that the old timers have been lying, ALL of them."

"Not all of them! The ones in prison, they originally told Dante about 'the great lie'. It's not all of them, Collin!"

Both Collin and Phillip understood the emotion behind Willows words. After all, both her parents went down into the great unknown and left her here, in the 'known of constant dread'. Collin could see the way Willow looked at the rope. Until he knew what was the truth, lie or no lie, he didn't want to see anyone else disappear into the fog. He had to be careful as he spoke to his friend.

Paradise Lost

"Your parents are probably dead!"- Philip.

He was never one for tact, which is why Collin didn't mind so much when people made fun of him. And, although his comment was completely inappropriate, it did get Willow to step away from the tree.

"I'm going home" She spoke softly, "Before I push Phil off the edge!" a mixture of spite, seriousness and humor were all evident in her tone.

Since the humor was still there, Collin knew she was okay.

"You don't want to go to The Tower?" Collin asked as she passed him by, "Most likely the Professor is there, he is always good for a laugh."

"You guys go ahead. It's getting cold out and I wouldn't want to catch FAT from Phillip."

"It's not a disease!" Philip shouted as she walked further away laughing as she went.

Collin waited long enough for her to be out of earshot before his big metal hand smacked Phillip upside his head.

"Ouch!!! What was that for?"
"'Your parents are probably dead'? What's the matter with you?"

"She had that crazy look in her eye; I didn't want her to jump down that rope! I mean you got to admit, Dante's scroll isn't all that believable either, what was it he said,

'A flood covered the world below, but those with strong enough ships rose to the heights of heaven, sadly to find it made of ash.' That's just too poetic to be true."

"You're every friend's worst enemy" Said Collin with a smile. "Let's go to The Tower."

ACT 1 SCENE 4: Meet Kaustos

"Before the beauty, must come the horror."- Solemn

Inside the jail you could feel the anticipation rising from the walls. Today was a day like no other, one that every imprisoned rebel had longed for since the loss of the war. Yes it was with eagerness and pangs that they sat in their cells, quietly listening for that dreadful screeching from the big Metal door.

SCREECH!

Solemn slowly appeared, causing shouts of applause to ring through every bar. He responded with a wave and a smile.

The guard came running towards the entrance.

"So you saw it!?" he asked.

"Yes, it looks spectacular!" Reaching into his tattered old pocket Solemn pulled out a small piece of paper, "It's almost yours, Lancer", dangling it in front of the guards face. "Now open up his cell."

Lancer looked towards the isolation room which held Kaustos "I…I just don't…"

"That wouldn't be wise." Said Solemn in a serious tone, "Think of your wife." he added clutching the paper, "Don't make me throw it off the edge of the world."

Shiloh Callaghan

As the other prisoners hooted and hollered, Lancer quickly regained his grit. "Right this way."

"Good choice."

They walked down the long narrow hallway leading to the rusty old door at the other end. The other inmates excitedly began to stomp in unison as the two men made their way down the aisle.

Boom! Booom! Booom!.... Boom! Boom! Boom!

"Here we are." Said the guard, having to raise his voice over the noise.

"Unlock it."

Boom Booom Booom!.... Boom Boom Boom!

CLUNK

As the door swung wide, a beastly looking shadow overwhelmed its frame. A little over 2 meters in height, he ducked down as he exited the cell.

Boom Booom Booom!.... Boom Boom Boom!

 Solemn: "It's good to see you again."

However, Kaustos was too incensed to respond to his comrade's greeting.

Paradise Lost

"What are you still doing here!?" he said, looking at Lancer (the guard).

"I was waiting for Solemn, I…"

"Solemn is here! Get to The Tower, you fool and find the boy!"

"Yes… if I can just have the keep-sake until it is time. That was our agreement."

Kaustos didn't hesitate to grab the much smaller man by his thin neck.

Boom Booom Booom!…. Boom Boom Boom!

Slamming the mans head into the rusted old door he barked, "You will get it when you bring me the boy. Now go!" Kaustos then shoved the guard to the floor.

Boom Booom Booom!…. Boom Boom Boom!

Kaustos: "It's good to see you too, brother!"

ACT 1 SCENE 5: TO THE TOWER WE GO

Walking to The Tower, the two boys rehashed a conversation that they shared a million times before; including such topics as,

Where do we come from?
What is our hope?
Is "the great lie" actually a lie?

And like every time before, they were sure that they could unlock the mysteries of their life in a 10 minute conversation.

"So we have two main philosophies" spoke Philip in his scholarly tone "first, the old people's story. I think it explains rather well why we are born with these clearly unnatural shackled, much better than Dante anyway."

"That's true" responded Collin with an equally sophisticated pitch "but like Dante said, where-ever these chains came from, THEIR existence was the catalyst for the great lie, if our shackles fell off we would find that our "powers of creation" and everything else was a hoax!"

"Removing the shackles is the key!" spoke Philip as if his brain struck some sort of untapped intellectual gold.

"Yes, but how? It's been tried many times before, Remember professor Murphy? I think we all learned a lesson from him."

Paradise Lost

"Yeah" responded Phil with a sigh "poor 'no- hands' Murphy."

Both looked down at their wrists and cringed.

"What about professor Stones theory?"

Collin gave a slight grin. Although it could not be seen under his metal mask, Philip knew it was there.

"I like how it tickles my ears, but it sounds..... Well..."

"Crazy?" said Philip, filling in the blank.

"Yes! I mean the idea that if all of us children learn how to dream, which is supposedly the first step to creation, THEN if one succeeds, his or her youthful power can free himself, who in turn...

"COULD FREE US ALL!" both shouted, gesticulating wildly as they mocked the old professor.

"It is funny" remarked Collin "Before Dante's scroll, we just believed whatever we were told without question. But now, it all sounds like utter nonsense."

"Well, I guess that's why Professor Stone wanted us to come here" said Philip. "It's the one mystery not even Dante dare explain or deny."

The two boys had arrived near the base of The Tower. Although old defaced and slowly grumbling away, one still couldn't help but be awestruck every time that they saw it.

Shiloh Callaghan

With a height that far surpassed any other structure left on the world, it seemed to loom over the boys as they looked up at it.

"How much do you think it weighs?" asked Philip.

"I don't know, maybe… 2 ½ Philips."

"Hahaha…jerk."

"The real question is, what do you think is holding it up?" asked Collin as he slowly stepped underneath the large stone base.

"Get out from under there!" said Phillip "It freaks me out every time someone does that."

Collin jumped out of the space feeling giddy from head to toe. "Wahoo! Come on, you're missing the best part of The Tower! Just try it once."

"No way!"

Well, how about YOU? YES YOU? Do YOU dare to try? It's not everyday that you can experience the thrill of standing beneath a hovering Tower. Come on, just for a second. They say a beautiful mosaic is painted underneath. It's worth the risk, trust me.

(Please choose one)

Yes I will go
(Continue reading)

Paradise Lost

No I am a scared little girl and I don't want my pretty pink dress to get dirty.
(If No, please go to The Table of Possible Context)

Yes, that's it, keep walking. Its amazing isn't it! Look at the detailed engravings that run up all four sides of The Tower. No one knows who created it, it has always been. See how each brick separately has its own personality, yet they still manage to make one beautiful design?

Okay, you're almost there. Can you see underneath? It's underbelly is domed, so YOU have to go all the way under if YOU want to see the mosaic. And… there.

"What is that!" said Collin, looking at YOU.

"What?" asked Phil.

"Under the Tower, It's like… something made of... water."

"If this is one of your stupid tricks to get me under the tower, it's not going to work."

"It's not a trick! Look, it moved!"

YOU should keep still.

"I don't see anything. Come on man, our homework is finished, stop playing around and let's go."

But Collin couldn't take his eyes off of YOU. "I think it's… looking at us."

Shiloh Callaghan

"Collin" said Philip with a more concerned tone "I am looking under the tower, there's nothing there, let's go."

Philip grabbed his friend by the shoulder trying to pull him away.

"It's right there!" said Collin as he brushed off Philips hand.

The fear in Collins voice gave a ring of truth to his words but as he looked again, Philip just couldn't see YOU. "What are you seeing?" he asked.

Collin stepped in closer, "I can't really explain it... but it's there. Why can't you see it?!" whispered Collin as he drew in a few meters away.

"Go get Professor Stone!"

"What? Why?"

"Just go and get him! I need someone who can explain this."

Phillip became more and more worried, "Collin, let's just go together, you can tell him yourself what you are seeing?"

"I am not going to take my eyes off of it! Just go, please. And hurry!"

Phillip took off, running through the maze of rubble that surrounded the tower.

Paradise Lost

Collin couldn't help but shake his head in irritation as he gradually heard his friends run turn into a trot and finally a brisk walk.

Collin picked up an old piece of rebar lying on the ground.

Slowly he is circling YOU, it is obvious that he is afraid but his curiosity far outweighs his fear. He wasn't going to leave, for after all, YOU were something new! YOU were something that was from a dream. Maybe YOU are the key to all the answers he has been looking for.

"What are YOU?"

Shiloh Callaghan

Paradise Lost

Act 2

*Second Law: The Creation of a human
life is only the image of that life. A soul
cannot be reanimated.*

ACT 2 SCENE 1: Introduction

Collin:

I know I am not crazy! I see YOU. Can YOU hear me? Can YOU understand my words?
(silence)… well no matter.

YOU don't seem real. Maybe this is a dream…Ouch! Okay I felt that pinch, it's not a dream.

Are YOU from below? Did someone create YOU?! Why couldn't Philip see YOU? Am I the only one?

"You're not the only one."

Collin quickly turned around to find one of the guards from the prison approaching The Tower.

"You can see it right!?" asked Collin desperately.

"Yes."

"Well, you're an old timer, what is it?!"

Giving YOU a long and hard look, Lancer replied,

"I don't exactly know, but I followed it here from the prison." He then turned to Collin as he spoke his next words, "Kaustos told me something was coming, he said I should tell him when I see.."

"Kaustos?! THE Kaustos?" interrupted Collin. "What did he say about it?!"

By now both of their eyes have shifted back onto YOU. The old guard cautiously looked around, "Not much, but he did say 'only one who has never dreamed would be ale to see it'. He mentioned that that one would be special. He said Collin would be special. That is your name, is it not?"

The boys mind began to race with a nervous dread. "You also can see it! I'm no different from you."

"That is where you are wrong. I have seen paradise, dreamt dreams. Something as majestic as this is in my realm of understanding, however it shouldn't be in yours."

Shiloh Callaghan

Collins curiosity was now overwhelmingly obvious. Lancer the guard knew now was the right time.

"However you aren't wrong to have questions. Kaustos knows much more than he was willing to share with me. But maybe he will be willing to talk to you" Said the guard as he came in close to Collins ear, "willing to share his secrets with the special child born from ash."

"But how? I'm not allowed in the prison."

"My shift doesn't end for another few hours. I can get you in boy. You, WE can find out what else he knows. I know, this all seems crazy, right?"

Even after Dante's scroll, Collin had no desire to ever go into the prison. Every time he walked by it, the building seemed to vibrate from his fright. But with YOU, things were different. Collin needed no further persuasion to risk a walk into the dark and unknown home of villainy. However fear still had a hold on him, he wasn't willing to go alone.

"Before we go, let's wait for The Professor and my friend, they will be here soon. Then we can all go."

The old guard immediately replied with a gruff "NO!" grabbing Collin by the shoulders he urged him "Kaustos and Professor Stone don't have the best of history. If we are to discover anything, we must go alone! We must go now!"

Collin could tell that the guard was nervous. Something didn't feel right. But how could he say no? Besides, except for Professor Stone and The Mayor, prison guards were the most trusted of men.

Giving YOU another look, his curiosity reached the stage of action.

"Let's go."

ACT2 SCENE2: Prison

When they had left The Tower, Collins mind began to bubble up with excitement. Although his history was of a paradise, Collin had only every seen bleakness, pain. As with many others he couldn't help but become frustrated at this obvious paradox. And sadly, hearing without ever seeing began to have a deafening effect.

SHOW ME,

This is what people wanted. And now Collin had seen miracles were possible. So maybe, paradise was also.

They arrived at the back gate of the prison a little before midnight. When Collin looked up at the creepy old structure, he knew tonight's nightmares would be some of the worst yet. It was a two-story mess of concrete, rust and mold lurking in the moonlight. The rickety old gate squeaked as the guard opened it, sending chills down Collin spine.

"Are you sure we won't get in trouble?" he whispered.

"From who? Don't worry, we are fine."

Collin however felt anything but fine. And as the old-timer unlocked the big front door Collin could feel a stiff breeze rushing out, escaping while it still could.

Lancer: "It's cold inside at night. No heat."

Paradise Lost

Shadows of bars drenched in moonlight scattered their way across the floor. Collin tried to gulp down his fear as he entered,

GULP! (It didn't work)

SLAM! The guard closed the door behind them.

The boy took his first few steps cautiously. Peeking in the nearby cells, he expected to find some sort of monster ready to pounce on him. But as they moved down the hallway, there were no monsters, not even people.

Drippings from old pipes rang in Collins ears, adding to the gloomy ambiance. It was spookier than the boy ever imagined. He began to wonder when a zombie was going to jump out and eat his brains.

"Where is everyone?" he asked.

"Um" answered the guard, desperately thinking of a lie. "I put them in one cell on the second floor at night, helps them stay warm. All except for Kaustos of course. He stays alone, always."

"Where?"

"End of the hallway, just behind that metal door."

Collin could see the door, with a figure in the window.

Tap, Tap, Tap

Shiloh Callaghan

As far as Collin was concerned, their footsteps started to thunder as they made their way down the corridor.

 A small circular window in the middle of the door framed-in a face with eyes looking out at Collin and the guard as they approached.

"He looks rough boy, be prepared."

Collin had seen pictures of Kaustos in Professor Stones class (be-it they were stick figures that the professor drawn), yet the hair was surprisingly accurate. Long and curly, shooting up and out as if struck by lightning.

When they reached the cell Kaustos stood away from the door.

Flick

The guard turned on the light switch.

The door slowly opened. Collin felt as if the top from an old treasure chest was being popped off before his very eyes. Except for guards, Dante was one of the few people who were ever allowed to visit with Kaustos. Growing up, he was just an evil ghost in stories but now he was real and he was standing before Collin, ready to speak.

"This is the boy?" he asked in a gruff voice.

"Yes" replied the guard.

Paradise Lost

Kaustos threw a roguish smile toward the guard, "Thank you, Lancer."

He turned his attention to Collin.

Looking at him from top to bottom he spoke, "So, you don't seem too afraid."

But Collin was.

And for the next few moments a chilled silence filled the small cell.

Collin tried his best to compile all his thoughts before he spoke. The question of YOU was just on the top of the list. Having the audience of Kaustos was rare and Collin wanted to make the best of it. Was the great lie a lie? What do you know about The Tower? Is there land below? Why do you know about me and that thing (YOU)? Anyone of these questions would have satisfied a part of Collin. However none of those questions were asked, and "What's the truth?!" seemed to be what blurted out of his mouth.

"Hahaha!" the old man let out a laugh that almost cracked his mask. "Well, isn't that the question everyone has... everyone except those who have SEEN the truth. Right, Lancer?"

The guard nodded in agreement.

"Leave me and the boy, Lancer, we will talk later."

"But..."

Shiloh Callaghan

"Leave us!" snapped Kaustos, sending Lancer in retreat. "From the looks of you, you must be about 16, right?"

"Yes."

"Well, before I educate you on the truth, why don't you educate me. At your age, you must be in old Stones class. So what did he teach you? What is the 'professors' idea of truth?"

Collin didn't exactly know where to began. His eyes shifted back and forth as if he was searching for the answer somewhere on the floor, all the meanwhile remaining silent.

The slight glow of happiness on Kaustos' face had faded. "Don't be simple-minded boy, answer the question!"

When Kaustos' voice grew, a fear gripped around Collins body, one which led to a rapid reply,

"What do you want to know?" he asked, trying his best to swallow down his fear.

"I have been in isolation a longtime, 1000 years, boy. I want to know…. everything. Let's start with the war." Kaustos took a seat on his bed as if awaiting a story.

Collin was almost certain that Kaustos already knew everything, but he didn't dare disappoint. Clearing his throat he began to speak "So, the war."

ACT2 SCENE3: The War

"I was taught that it began… with you. Professor Stone said you were the first to break the divine law and not 'create with love.'"

Kaustos grinned, "Continue, boy."

"A seed of evil then grew inside of you, one you could have cut away but didn't. You wanted it to grow." Collin finally began to look at Kaustos in his eyes as he continued to speak, "This wickedness eventually took root in your creations. You became destructive, violent, evil. Thus the name we all call you, Kaustos, evil one."

"Interesting." He replied as one heavy hand cracked the knuckles of the other, "But If I was this… Evil with unlimited power, why didn't I just kill everyone before they knew what was happening? What has professor Stone said about that?"

"You wanted to win a battle of ideals. Killing everyone would just make you alone. But changing peoples thinking would give you followers, give you power. Love is weak and slow but Pride is strong and fast, better for advancement. That's what we were told you believe." Collin paused to take a breath. "At least that's what I was told."

Cocking his head to the right, Kaustos looked extremely displeased. However he wouldn't deny nor confirm anything. He simply said, "Continue."

Shiloh Callaghan

"Many agreed with you. At the end almost one third of the whole world did." Collin gave a brief smile, hoping that statement would lighten some of the tension he felt in that prison cell. It didn't. "But then they, not you...well, okay also you, I mean, The Professor said to prove your point you created creatures of great power, creatures he called Flaksens. They destroyed anything that had been created by hands or tongues. A civilization that took Love from the beginning of time to build, Pride and strength tore down in a day… and that was when the fighting began."

Kaustos slowly replied in his raspy voice, "I can see why you are nervous around me. I have been made into the father of all evil. But do you believe it boy?"

He hesitated before answering , "Well I..."

"You don't know, do you?" interrupted Kaustos "After all, how could you? In your little story I didn't once hear the voice of a child but only a regurgitated sermon from a crazy old Professor. Actual thinking, you should try it before you speak. Then again that could cause you to end up in here." Kaustos sighed, hoping for a hint of doubt and compassion from Collin. "So tell me, how does the fairytale of 'the great lie' end?"

"The creators of love had no choice but defend themselves from the Flaksens, they never instigated a fight..."

"Hah!" huffed Kaustos, unable to control himself. Collin pretended not to notice as he continued to speak,

Paradise Lost

"...Sadly, no one, including you, knew the secret our world held. No one knew it was mostly a creation of hands and tongue. When The Flaksen sunk their teeth into the ground... everyone, everything just dropped below the fog. All but this small patch of real land became a victim of your creation".

Kaustos next few words seemed to roar out of his mouth, "And why would I want that!? Stone, that ignorant old fool, teaching slanderous beliefs and murdering my character! Why would I be so careless boy! Do I look like a stupid idiot to you!?"

Collin thought it best not to answer.

"Don't bother with the rest of the story! Dante already told me what lies were being spewed out at that school. Three words as why I didn't supposedly stop it! Three! What are they, go on, say em'?

Collin hoped what he was about to say was right, "No one knows?"

Already roused Kaustos jolted near Collin. "That's right! No one knows! How could they say I am responsible for such an irresponsible act which killed millions!? No one knows, well I know something that no one knows! I know about YOU!"

Kaustos' eyes looked away from Collin and were staring at YOU. Look boy, you can see IT, can't you? IT'S right there!?"

Shiloh Callaghan

Collin turned around and looked a few meters away. Jumping back out of shock, he nervously spoke, "What is IT? How did IT come inside?"

"What is IT? THAT is freedom!"

ACT2 SCENE4: Freedom

"Now it's my turn to explain the truth, Clone!"

"It's Collin."

"Whatever! Listen good, everything you have been told, is absolute fantasy! And if an old-timer like me chooses to speak up, we get locked away in this horrible place. 'The Great Lie' is just that, it's a lie! And now I can prove it! We can prove it! We just needed to wait for THAT THING so others will believe."

Collin started to likes the idea of being in a "we" sentence with an important person, especially when he was a savior. And seeing YOU gave him great confidence in the so-called 'evil man' standing before him.

Kaustos continued to speak, however this time he sounded far more elegant, "'Two who can see, one who can dream and the other who believes, if both touch the unseen, all will be set free.' You understand, boy!?"

The blank look on Collins face gave an affirming NO. Leaning in closer to him, Kaustos explained, "A longtime ago, I discovered those words, among others. 'Two who can see' this THING, me and you boy. 'One who can dream' (Kaustos pointing to himself), and finally 'the other who believes'… you.

Shiloh Callaghan

If we just touch that unseen, it will set me free!"

"All free." responded Collin.

"What?" replied Kaustos with a whisper of hate.

"Before you said 'ALL will be set free'."

"Oh Yes, yes Of course! All we need to do is touch it, and these shackles will be gone for good! Come on Boy!" urged Kaustos as he grabbed Collin by his shirt.

Collin was being yanked towards YOU, until his shuffling feet firmly planted themselves into the ground.

"Wait!" He said with a bit of panic. "Why is it so important to release these Shackles? Why not go down the tree with Dante, didn't you tell him that's where freedom lies?"

Kaustos could see the wheels of reason start to spin slowly in Collins mind. Either truth or a lie, he needed to give the boy a reason to believe (italics) . For this to work, Collin has to believe. Thinking for a moment, Kaustos opted for something in-between.

"Your parents, do you remember them?"

"What?" asked Collin, a bit confused by the question.

"They most likely died when you were very young, as do most from every generation but mine. So I ask you again, do you remember them?"

Paradise Lost

"No" replied Collin. "But I have a keepsake of them. One The Mayor made for me, so I know what they look like."

"It's a sad thing, isn't it? Something about raising a baby in this horrible world, maybe that's what kills most of them so young."

"Why are you telling me this?" Asked Collin.

Kaustos reached in his Pocket and took out a small piece of paper. He unraveled it. "Are you ready to hear something new?"

"Yes" he answered while looking at the picture.

"The Tower holds many secrets boy; one just needs the cipher to discover them. Tell me what you see?"

Collin looked down at a rather rudimentary drawing.

"It's of a man without shackles. He's standing above a grave."

"Yes, but look closer! What else can you see?"

Collin focused all he could on the old crumpled-up piece of paper.

"There is a hand... coming out of the grave."

"Yes! Honestly, what could it mean?"

Shiloh Callaghan

If there was ever a time for Collin to doubt, this should have been it. There were so many things that Collin should have considered, like, 'anyone could have drawn this,' or 'why didn't he show the drawing to Dante? But sadly, he didn't. The rush of possibilities, mixed with the miracle of YOU were too enticing for clear thinking. Collin, if only for a moment, believed. And Kaustos wasted no time bringing him near.

Collin: "Resurrection!?"

Choose:

Let them touch you (keep reading)

Run away before they have the chance! (please go to The Table of Possible Context)

Paradise Lost

Shiloh Callaghan

Act 3

*Third Law: The power you hold within
is mighty, yet in the face of organic
elements it will prove scanty.*

ACT3 SCENE1: Introduction

Kaustos:

So, YOU'RE The Observer. You're not as … MUCH as I imagined. I am curious what YOU actually consider YOURSELF? Good? Evil? maybe something in-between. Well, whatever it is, I would like to assure YOU of something. YOUR irrelevance. Hate me or love me, in the end it makes no difference. I have read the secrets of The Tower and I already know the outcome.

Now YOU, YOU may think YOU'RE safe, safe to watch and unravel the epic days to come without a hint of danger posed to YOU. Good, YOUR ignorance pleases me. But before this story is through, YOU also will…

Shiloh Callaghan

"Excuse me, sir… my wife. Please, you promised…"

Kaustos' eyes shifted from YOU, to the pitiable looking guard, "you dare interrupt me!?" He shrieked.

"I'm sorry" pleaded Lancer, "I just want the keep-sake and its realization, then I will leave you."

Kaustos grunted angrily, "Let me give YOU an idea of the wonders to come". Thrusting his hand in his pocket he took out another piece of paper. Giving Lancer a look of disgust, Kaustos whispered the word "life" over it as he held it in his now bare hand.

Lancer looked down at the picture with great excitement. She was beautiful, just as he remembered her from long ago, before the war. He never actually expected Kaustos to do it, just having the picture would have been payment enough.

He watched a slight shine of blue energy encircle the keep-sake. It was really happening! And Lancers tearful eyes looked on in ecstasy at the amazement to come. This wasn't the first person he had seen made into their own image, but it was the most important one.

Small specks that look like stars will soon appear, swirling in the blue energy. The beautiful sound of flowing water. A mist will emerge in the air, outlining the body. And finally, YOU will see her, breathing and teeming with energy.

Just like he remembered, every step appeared before his teary eyes. The stars, the sound and the mist all built up

Paradise Lost

anticipation for the spectacular finally. Lancer knew she wasn't a soul, she didn't posses REAL life. But in this horrible be-darkened world, there was his wife. She was beautiful, perfect.

Sadly though, the director of this miracle doesn't like beautiful endings.

"Say hello!" Kaustos shouted, crumpling up the keep-sake and throwing it into the air.

From that point on, time seemed to stop. Lancer looked in absolute shock at his wife slowly materializing, flailing upward in the air. His scream only made Kaustos grin that much wider, showing off every one of his black teeth.

The woman YOU now see falling is named Heaven. She was wearing the same beautiful white dress on the day that she died. Time unfroze and Lacers watched in horror as she came crashing down to a dismal end.

The guard looked towards Kaustos, whose hand was now stretching out towards him.

Kaustos: "Your turn!"

Shiloh Callaghan

ACT3 SCENE2: Back in the classroom

"See… he's not dead! He is just sleeping on my desk, like a handsome prince ready to be kissed and awoken by 7 dwarf-women!" The Professor smiled as he reassured Philip of his friends safety.
However, Philip just became more confused.

"Collin! Collin!" He ran towards the desk and shook Collin until he awoke. "Are you okay?"

"Yes, I'm fine." he drowsily answered while giving a morning stretch.

It took a few seconds for the events from the previous day to be recalled. 3 seconds to be exact.

3,2,1,

"Yes!!!!! I am better than okay!" Jumping up in excitement he gave a joyous cry "I am free! Look free!"

Collin thrillingly showed off his hands, ready to hear sounds of shock and awe.

However, the only thing he heard came from Philip and although it sounded like the word awe, its meaning was very different.

"Uh?"

Paradise Lost

Collin focused in on the metal gloves still banded onto his hands. "This is imposable, it doesn't make any sense! Last night we were free, I saw his hands with my very eyes!"

"You dreamed of being free?!" exclaimed Stone. He found this quit a break-through in his theory, which led to an eruption of excitement, "Wahoo!!!!!!!!!! This is the first step! Don't you see! Don't you both see? The first dream from a non-dreamer. Your generation's consciousness is finally being affected. This is...Awesome!"

"What are you talking about!?" asked Collin with a tone of frustration. "It wasn't a dream! And what I saw yesterday wasn't a vision, it was real! Why is this cursed mask back on!?"

"Outstanding!" answered The Professor, still not believing a word Collin said, "It seemed so real, you can't even tell the difference. Next time you dream try kissing the palm of your hand, it's the next best thing to kissing a real woman! That is unless there is a woman in the dream, then... well... you know what to do, also..."

"Idiot!" replied Collin. "I was free! Kaustos was free and THAT THING was no vision!"

"Kaustos was also free!?" guffawed Philip, "Right, now I know you're joking. I think..."

"Quiet!" Professor Stone felt an immediate sickening in his stomach. "How was he freed!?"

Shiloh Callaghan

The Professor's fun-loving spirit quickly extinguished. Collin could see that he finally got the man's attention. "THE... THING. We touched it, Kaustos knew it would free us. He knows a lot of things Professor."

"What did he tell you Collin?"

"About 'The Great Lie.' It is true, isn't it? There was never a paradise?"

"Collin..." The Professor tried to answer his student, but the boy wouldn't allow room for it,

"He didn't just speak! He showed me the truth!"

"And how did he do that?"

"By showing me his face, without a mask! Sure, a mouth isn't as pretty as I thought it would be, ugly black teeth and all, but he showed me. What have you ever showed us?"

The Professor again tried to reply, But Collin bulldozed straight through his words, "After I saw him free, His hands touch shackles...I was free....I felt them come off. Then I...I don't really remember. You woke me up... But it wasn't a dream!"

Twisting one of the two braids that hung from his bearded chin The Professor mulled over what he heard. "Hmmm...me and Philip went looking for you at The Tower, you weren't there."

Paradise Lost

"Like I said, I went to the prison! A guard named Lancer took me there," Collin suddenly burst with an eager excitement, "Ask him! He will prove that it wasn't a dream! He saw IT too!"

"Lancer? He is a good man" Said the Professor. "And by IT, I assume you are referring to what you saw with Philip?

Collin looked pleased that The Professor didn't say "what you believe you saw with Philip," but actually put a little trust in him.

"Yes," he replied.

 "Philip, put a sign on the door, class is canceled today."

"Canceled? Why?"

"We are taking a little field trip."

ACT3 SCENE3: The Field trip

As the walked, The Professor had Collin explain in detail everything that he saw and heard from the night before. Amid the conversation, anyone in earshot could hear a high amount of hostility coming from Collin.

"Why are you speaking so rudely?" asked Philip.

Mean-mugging The Professor, Collin spoke,
"Haven't you been listening, haven't you both been? I know the great lie was a Lie! The second I saw Kaustos' shackles fall from his hands, I knew what he said was true!"

"Then why are your shackles still there?" asked Philip mockingly.

"Shut-up!"

In a soft tone, The Professor decided to rejoin the conversation "Seeing isn't always believing, right?" Surprisingly he was coming to Collin's defense.

"Yes!" agreed Collin.

"Yes to what?" asked the Professor.

"Yes, seeing isn't always believing!" restated Collin with conviction.

"And up has a down, in an out, left it's right, girl her boy, and fiddle its faddle, you see?"

Paradise Lost

Collin was never more confused in his life, "What are you talking about?"

"Me and Philip didn't see, so we don't believe even though it may be true, yes? Well you saw so you believe, even though it may not be true! fiddle, faddle my boy!...("What's a faddle?" said Philip)... In other words, don't be so sure that everything Kaustos said and showed you was true. That is, if it wasn't a dream, which I am sorry to disappoint you, but I highly believe it was."

"Why do you refuse to believe me?" complained Collin.

The professor looked into his eyes, "Because you are still alive."

Just ahead was the Prison entrance, Philip spoke up "Well, we will soon find out."

As they approached the Prison, Stone was watching carefully for anything out of the ordinary. If Kaustos was free there would be signs of it, maybe an unbarred window, not enough guards or something like a flying fire breathing death monster. Anything at all that would prove what Collin said to be true. But everything looked the same.

"Morning Stone" greeted one of the guards at the entrance. "What can we do for you?"

"You haven't seen any flying fire breathing death monsters, have you?"

Shiloh Callaghan

"Umm… no, can't say that I have." chuckled the guard.

"Ah, that's good to know" responded The Professor with a smile. "Then how about Lancer, is he here?"

"Sure, he is inside, let me go get him for you."

(Horn noise in the distance)

As the guard walked away, Collin's face began to bubble with excitement. "He will tell you!"

It wasn't long before the door to the prison opened and out came Lancer.

"Lancer!" screamed Collin "I hear the horn, you must have told everyone about what we saw! About Kaustos!"

However as he slowly drew near, an obvious look of bewilderment became clearer and clearer.

"Stone, why is this orphan talking to me?"

"I thought you knew each other?" said The Professor.

"Everyone knows everyone nowadays, but I've never had a conversation with the boy. Hey young man, what are you rambling about?"

Collin was stunned. He didn't know how to respond. He just stood there looking lost.

Paradise Lost

The Professor tried his best to help out. "This is my finest student! The first non-dreamer to have not only a dream, but also a vision! Apparently your rugged hobo style also inspired him. You were a character in his dream, isn't that exciting Lancer?!"

"Really boy!? You dreamt about something good!? That's amazing! What was it?"

"It wasn't... I was free... you were there." Collin was having a hard-time grasping the truth that was presented to him. "No! it was real! Kaustos, I spoke to him. I came inside this prison, you brought me in here!"

Lancer gasped, "Sorry boy but that's impossible. Ever since Kaustos spread those lies to Dante, only old-timers have been allowed in the prison, you are mistaken. Don't worry, sometimes my dreams can be pretty vivid too. But this is good news, if your Professors idea about your generation and dreaming is true, you must be very special, Collin."

(Horn noise in the distance)

"Hey Stone, what are they blowing that horn for this time?" asked Lancer.

"Who knows why they ever blow that stupid thing" responded The Professor.

"Actually everyone should know" eagerly spoke Philip who was dying to enter the conversation. "There must be an important announcement."

Shiloh Callaghan

"We all know that, pudgy" said Lancer. "But what's the important announcement about?"

Seeing as how Philip barely knew the man, that insult actually hurt. "Well, I don't know" he responded rather dejectedly.

"Why don't we go and check it out, boys" said The Professor, "Lancer, it was really nice seeing you again."

Lancer reached out to meet The Professors hand, "good to see you too."

"Mmm… you know what boys, why don't you go ahead, I will stay here with Lancer."

"What for!?" responded all three at once.

"I want to talk to Kaustos, see what he has to say."

Lancer was quick to respond "I don't think that's a good idea."

"Why not? It will only be for a short while." Looking towards the boys he spoke to Philip "Take your friend and go."

"But professor!" Urged Collin "I…"

"Just go, Collin, I will find out if there is anything more than a dream to this story."

Paradise Lost

As Philip pulled Collin away, he turned back towards Lancer "I know it was true!"

ACT3 SCENE4: A red balloon

"Move it, you old fart!" said Willow with sass whilst elbowing an old man out of her way. The horn blew again, this time louder than before. "It better not be another food shortage announcement," she thought as she made her way to the front of the stage. It seemed like everyone in the town/ city /world (take your pick) was there. Willow hoped to run into Collin or Philip among the crowed, but unbeknown to her they had just left the prison.

"Well I could go stand with some of the other girls" said Willow to herself, "but they would just ask me 'why aren't you with your boyfriend Collin?'… then I would puke out of my nose onto their faces! No, better I stay here."

She turned back to the stage to see one of the old-timers walking onto it. "Attention! Attention! Our Mayor has an announcement of vital importance. Please listen carefully, thank you."

"Oh no! It is another food shortage!" thought Willow.

The crowed stared at the tattered old curtain in the background waiting for the Mayor to walk through it. Several minutes passed as everyone anticipated his entrance. Finally the crowed began to hear the Mayor's voice over the speakers surrounding the stage.

This was most unusual. Even the smallest amount of energy was to be saved for absolute emergencies, not for a stupid

Paradise Lost

62

speech about another bad harvest. With ears now burning, Willow along with everyone else was taking note of every word that came out of the speakers.

"My friends, my brothers, my sisters. Today is a day unlike any other in the history of our people. In times past we have had many joyous days and recently, far too many sad ones. And although we have tried our best to keep our hope, until today it has been in vain. Until today! (Very melodramatically spoken) Hope has for the first time risen from the ashes, or to be more accurate, from beneath them!"

The Mayor's body parted the curtain with one long stride. As he emerged onto the stage there was something bobbing behind him. When the old-timers caught sight of it, they gasped with amazement. However, the younger ones hadn't a clue what it was.

"What in the world is that thing!?"

"I don't know, I've never seen it before." responded Willow. "Hey, there you are!" She turned around towards Colin. "Look, it's floating on some sort of string!"

"A few hours ago," continued the Mayor, "this balloon was discovered attached to a ring around Dante's rope. And with it, this note…"

The crowed stood in amazement. It was as if their heads were snow globes and their ideas of life had just been violently shaken. The old-timers seemed more confused than the youngsters. They KNEW the war was true, they

Shiloh Callaghan

KNEW the rest of their world was ripped away. How could this be?

"…it reads,

'Dear friends, all that Kaustos spoke was true! The water has long dissipated and this world is magnificent. When we first arrived, it was an untamed paradise, a place of wild new trees, fruits and vegetables. Although some are hard to snort through the nose, their taste is amazing!

Haha!

Slowly we have been doing our best to bring the world back to the way it was and we are making good progress. Unfortunately we haven't found a way to remove our shackles yet but I am confident we will. We are discovering new things every day; old buildings, objects and engravings. We have tried rigorously to send word and we hope this time we are successful. If you receive this message, please join us immediately! The trip down the rope is long but manageable.

Your   friend   /hero
Dante '

I know what most of you are thinking, especially the old-timers, like me. How is this possible?

This question has puzzled me all morning." The Mayor paused in a moment of reflection. "There is one plausible scenario. The Flaksen. We know of the carnage they unleashed. We SAW it. However, when they burrowed

Paradise Lost

through the earth, digging and dissolving the world around us, what did we actually see? Do you remember? I do.

We saw nothing.

We heard the thunder and screams of a world dying and dropping all around but we saw nothing. A cloud of fog enveloped us while everything else went crashing down. What if... what if Kaustos wanted The Flaksen, not to destroy the world, rather to hide it? How else could we receive this message?"

A tremendous gasp roared through the crowed.

"Pure conjecture!" shot out one angry voice fallowed by a hum of agreement.

The Mayor could understand the old-timers disdain for any speech which didn't vilify Kaustos to the full degree. After all, he was the cause of everything and since everything was pain, well, you get the picture.

"You're right my friends, it is." Continued The Mayor "But this balloon, this note, they are not! Look, I abhor Kaustos as much as the rest of you. But I did not say what I did to promote him as a lesser evil, rather so as to bring hope! Hope of our freedom!"

The crowed quieted down as they contemplated The Mayor's words.

"What do you propose?" another old timer shouted.

Shiloh Callaghan

"It's been a longtime since Kaustos has been allowed to speak in a public forum. Once he discovers this message from Dante he will no doubt have something to say." Surveying his audience The Major gauged their response, "What say you?!"

It took a few seconds but a trickling applause soon turned into a thunderous one, giving a loud and clear "YES!"

"We will not allow this Villain to spread anymore lies or doubts in secret! He will have to face all of us... (Crowed cheering in agreement)... and like times past, love will prevail! As your mayor, I assure it, or my name isn't Solemn the great!"

ACT3 SCENE5: Back in the clink

"Opening it up!" Shouted Lancer as he waited for Kaustos to back away from his cell door. "You got a visitor, you sorry sack of filth!" he shouted as the heavy door screeched opened.

Both men came into each others view. At first neither man said a word. Standing directly parallel from the other, they spoke in looks, ones which told of battles from long ago.

Finally, Kaustos broke the silence,
"You've aged well, kind of like a smelly old cheese."

Stone tried to think of a witty comeback, but the only thing that came to mind was "Shut-up Poop-face!" Not the most eloquent of words. So The Professor decided it would be best to forgo the insult session and get straight to the point.

"Still wearing your mask and shackles?"

Kaustos smirked. "Professor, you're becoming delusional in your old age, if you haven't noticed everyone has these cursed things."

"You know, I believed the boy was having a dream, I was almost certain," He continued as he pointed at Lancer "until your friend here gave it away. Do yourself a favor, next time you create an image spend more time on it, this ones too hollow."

Shiloh Callaghan

The guard immediately interrupted, "Professor, what are you babbling about, you need to leave (THUD!) imm...!"
Slowly the guard looked down to find The Professors fist inside his chest cavity. Lancers body slowly changed to the color of ash as it began to crumple onto the floor.

"Oops! I think I broke it" said The Professor, shaking the dust off of his hand.

"You always have to be so darn theatrical, don't you!" growled Kaustos as he waved his hand, putting Lancer back together. Stone watched as Kaustos mask and shackles faded. "So, how did you find out? What gave it away?"

"When I shook its hand. There was no life in it, no weight."

"Well, I need to store power, I didn't bother with the details." Responded Kaustos as he clinched his hand, crushing Lancers image once again.

"You always have trouble with the details, just like during the war."

"Maybe" responded Kaustos, raising the image of Lancer once again. "Or I could be too focused on the unseen, the big picture which only I can perceive. That tends to distract me from the little things"

Kaustos flung his hand opened, this time exploding Lancers image all over Professor Stone.

The Professor coughed out dust as he replied, "Little things... like peoples lives?"

Paradise Lost

"Exactly."

"Do you mind?"

"Of course!" responded Kaustos rather cordially as he spun his finger around, collecting the ash off of Stones face. "How should I kill it this time?"

"You can't kill an image," remarked Stone "It's not alive. However you could kill a boy. One who is apparently very special… yet you didn't. Why?"

"Mmm… you still haven't been able to solve the riddle of The Tower, hey Stone? Let's just say he is part of the big unseen picture."

"And me?" Asked The Professor with a hint of fear, "Is that why I haven't been eaten by a flying Hippo-souras? Or burned to death by an evil fem-oven on her period? Am I part of this picture?"

"Ha!" laughed Kaustos "I do admit, I used to love your creations, they were always so… absurd. You? You are indeed part of the picture." Kaustos again raised the image of Lancer. "But he wasn't. ERASE!" yelled Kaustos as the walls around him disappeared. "Neither were any of these poor men."

The Professor looked at the other prisoners, the rebels. And as Kaustos waved his hand from left to right, he watched their images all crumble away.

Shiloh Callaghan

"Don't look at me like that" spoke Kaustos nonchalantly, "they were just details, far too many loose ends. You know Stone, I never wanted to be loved and followed by my men," he explained while bringing back the images. "I just want to be followed."

The Professor was horrified, but not surprised. "Too what end?"

"I will tell you. But only if you answer one of my questions."

"Agreed" responded The Professor, all the while hoping the question wasn't "are you wearing underwear today?"

Kaustos walked close to him and leaned in "Was it you?"

"Me? Me what?"

"You know what!" answered Kaustos. "The shackles! It had to be someone clever enough to create something that my Flaksen couldn't destroy! And no-one else would be mad enough to take away everyone's powers, no-one except maybe you."

The professor gave his answer some thought. "The Tower didn't tell you?"

"No! Why do you think I am asking you!?" exploded Kaustos, obliterating Lancers image once more. He looked long and hard into the eyes of The Professor. "Then who?"

Paradise Lost

Stones voice slightly shook as he replied "The creator of The Tower."

"Yes… I suppose. After all it would have taken hundreds of years to store enough power that could Shackle everyone for this long." Kaustos took a moment to reflect "You know, I am surprised you discovered the truth so soon. It will all be over very quickly then." Kaustous stepped away from his visitor, "If you will excuse me." Snapping his fingers, he revealed a door, "See you again real soon Old Cheese."

The Professor knew that was his queue to leave. To go where-ever was on the other side of that opening. As he walked towards the light that burst through the doorway he remembered Kaustos owed him an answer to a question. "To what end do you want to be followed?"

"The only end," Kaustos replied with a black teeth smile. "One that leads back to the beginning."

Shiloh Callaghan

ACT3 SCENE6: The short march

"All I'm saying is, calling yourself 'Solemn the great' is tacky! I mean, am I right?"

Neither Collin nor Willow responded to Philips warranted attack on Solemn's character, both were lost in thought.

Willow could only think about one thing, making it down the rope and seeing her parents again. She was sure that they were alive and at this point she could care less about the great lie, the truth or anything in-between.

As for Collin, he still looked shell shocked. He gazed about, left and right through the crowed searching for something.

"Okay, I know Solemn didn't give himself that title 'the great', everyone else did but you don't call yourself that in public...hello? Is anyone listening, I feel like I am talking to myself."

Willow turned towards Philip with a look of disgust, "I just found out my parents are still alive and Collin is seeing some invisible thing which I am still not sure how that's even possible but nonetheless he see's it! Look around Philip! As we speak our whole civilization is walking to the worlds end to send a message to those below whilst we await the arrival of the worlds greatest evil/freedom fighter, Kaustos. (Leaning in closer)Do you think now is the time to care if the Mayor called himself 'the great' or not? Hmmm fatty?"

Paradise Lost

"...So you were listening." He responded with a smile. Turning his attention towards Collin, Philip saw his friend scanning away in search for YOU, or so he thought. "Didn't find IT yet?"

"I'm not looking for an IT," responded Collin "but a him. There!"

Collin bolted off through the crowed, pushing and shoving until he made his way towards the front, towards Solemn.

"Solemn!" he shouted from behind, however there was no response. Collin tried again, "Mr. Mayor!" still no response. "Oh for goodness sake! Solemn the great!"

Whipping his arrogance through the air, The Mayor turned around and finally responded, "Yes?"

"Hello, my name is Collin, I..."

"Oh yes, Collin. The dreamer!"

"What?" shockingly replied Collin.

"I have just heard a lot about you from my good friend Lancer! This must also be announced. What a glorious day my young friend!"

Collin looked angrily towards Lancer (technically his image),

"Stop pretending that yesterday never happened!"

Shiloh Callaghan

"Oh, calm down young man! Me and The Mayor were just discussing why your dream seemed so real to you."

"Yes" continued the Mayor, "This is your very first dream, young man, we believe it's hard for you to separate the two worlds. Your experience is unlike any other persons."

"What are you talking about?" replied Collin, "all of you old-timers dream."

"Yes, but you see me and Lancer have dreamt from the time that we were babies. We gradually were able to separate a dream from reality before we could even question if they were the same thing or not. But you, you are almost a full grown man who has only known the real world, so how could you tell the difference?"

Somehow, that logic seemed to hit Collin. Along with everyone else's doubt, he didn't know what to believe. "But I have had nightmares before, I always do. I can tell the difference. Aren't dreams the same feeling?"

The Mayor spoke with a tone of assurance in his next lie, "No. A Nightmare is based in fear, a relatively weak emotion. But a dream is based on the most powerful of all emotions, love. Just as opposite as a dream is from a nightmare, so are the experiences of each?"

"When do you think I will be able to dream again?" Collin asked, now mostly unsure of himself

"That's something I wanted to talk to you about" replied the Mayor. "What if your dear Professor is correct? What if your dream's can lead to a belief and that belief to a creation? You could help free us all!"

"That would be amazing." Answered Collin, still a little bewildered.

"It would be" Replied Solemn. He then put something in Collins hand. "I want you to go home and take this, it will help you sleep, maybe even dream."

"What is it?" asked Collin as he held up a vile.

"It's a small potion I made with different roots and plants, Just drink it through the nose before you lay down and you will fall fast asleep."

The Mayor and Lancer then gave the boy a look of 'get going kid!'

"You mean now!?" exclaimed Collin. "But look around…"

"Exactly!" interrupted Solemn. "Take a look round. We are about to reply to a world which was once thought of as lost, people whom we thought were dead seem to be alive! How wonderful would it be if we could give those ones an even greater surprise than the one they gave us, freedom!? Please, you must try and dream again!?"

Collin looked at the hopeful faces of the 2 men. He wanted what The Mayor said to come true. However with all the excitement and happiness around him, he couldn't help but want to stay.

Shiloh Callaghan

"So what's going to happen when I leave?" he asked with a slight frown.

Solemn took a piece of paper out of his pocket to show Collin.

"I will attach this note to something weighty and send it down the rope. We hope that someone down below will soon find it and send up a reply."

"And what about Kaustos, will I miss hearing what he has to say?" asked Collin.

"I am afraid so, he is on the way as we speak young man." With a smile Solemn continued "Don't worry so much, we will tell you all about it when you awake."

Collin gave a sad nod of agreement and began to walk away.

"Don't forget to shove that liquid up your nose before you sleep!" added Lancer.

"Okay."

Both man and Image watched as Collin fumbled back through the crowed.

"Well, that was easier than I thought!" said Solemn. "How much longer until he finds out it's all a lie?"

Lancer looked back at Solemn and replied in a different voice, in Kaustos voice "Not sure, but according to The Tower, whenever he does, it will be too late."

Paradise Lost

Shiloh Callaghan

Act 4

Fourth law: Any creation of an element will maintain its fundamental qualities, however lacking its innate power held within

Paradise Lost

ACT4 SCENE1: Introduction

Professor Stone:

It's You! How awesome it is to be in YOUR presence! YOU remind me of something special, something that was once very dear to me. Before, I created a whole civilization, all very similar to YOU. They were much smaller of course, all miniatures, but they had the same shimmer, the same watery hue. I made them all smell like blueberries... I don't suppose you do?

(Sniff!) NO, YOU smell more like...cinnamon. Anyway, I kept them on an island in the sky. But that was before The Flaksen found them... Those wretched creatures found everything!

So, I suppose YOU don't come from my little civilization or from this one either.

Well, what do YOU think of our world, this stage of fallen angels?

No response. That's okay. However I am rather curious why YOU are here, is it to help us regain our wings so to speak, or help Kaustos finish us all off?

Shiloh Callaghan

He stood smiling at you for a few minutes. It was a little creepy.

"Well, on with it!" he said again as his focus shifted above you to The Tower.

"Why would Kaustos send me here?" he asked aloud, slowly studying it. "He knows I have studied this structure for years without success, So why would today be any different?"

The Professor took a moment in thought. He then looked back down to YOU.

"YOU can make it different! But how?" He now began to examine you. This time his look was slightly creepier than before.

Slowly he approached. "Don't be afraid."

A rusty old shackle reached out toward YOU as The Professor looked up at the symbols on The Tower.

"YOUR hand feels like the soft hair of a woman" he said with a smile (Extremely creepy). "But touching YOU doesn't seem to help de-code anything." He removed his hand from yours. "You have to be able to help me somehow. Me and Kaustos used to be collogues you know" he said while examining YOU for more clues. "He was always a bit of a downer even before his whole apocalyptic act. Constantly looking at things only from his perspective, his... angle." The Professor let out a gasp. "Please come stand near me!?"

Paradise Lost

Please Choose one
Yes, I want to help. (please continue reading)

No, creepy old man, get away from me! (Please go to The Table of Possible Context)

As YOU approached, Professor Stone gleefully cried out "This is going to be interesting for us both! Now, please stand in front of me and look up at The Tower."

After listening to his request, The Professor spoke gently "Continue to look up. Oh! and don't scream or blow a whistle for help." With his eyes closed, he pressed his face into the watery back of your head.

It feels gross, doesn't it?

His eyes opened. At first the symbols and numbers all looked exactly the same as before, only now they were incased in YOUR water-like head. With no change, Professor Stone was about to scratch the idea. That was until things suddenly began to move. It was amazing actually, the fixed pictures moved with the other pictures, and the symbols with symbols until they all became a coherent looking mosaic, similar to the one at the base of The Tower. And in the next blink of The Professors eyes, the walls became written script (However the mosaic at the base remained the same). He quickly took his head out of sync with yours and looked towards The Tower,

"Awesome!" he exclaimed "Only through your eyes, only through your eyes!" he yelled.

Shiloh Callaghan

Ducking his head back into YOURS, he began to read all the things written on The Towers walls.

Paradise Lost

ACT4 SCENE2: 30 minutes later

The professor had finished reading. He found himself lost in thought over the discoveries he had made. One in particular rested on the tip of his tongue,

"YOU… YOU were here before!"

ACT4 SCENE3: The Boo's of the crowed

As Kaustos made his way threw the crowds, it was hard to believe that this society was once completely based off of love. Sentiments such as "Throw him off the cliff!" and "Use his face for a toilet!" came from every direction. However after the pain that most of them have endured, resentment could only be expected from the old-timers.

The younger generation held more of a puzzled feel than an angry one.

They just wanted to know what was the real truth to everything. And as they watched Kaustos being escorted towards Dante's rope, they highly anticipated an answer before casting any sort of judgment.

The mayor gestured to the crowed for silence, for Kaustos explanation was about to began.

If you liked Kausots or hated him, you wanted to listen to what he had to say. And as this symbol of so much controversy faced the crowds, an absolute silence echoed through everyone's ears, all patiently awaiting his address.

Looking out at all those eager eyes, Kaustos felt the one thing he missed the most since the loss of his abilities, power. When he opened his shackled (fake) mouth to speak he couldn't help but smile, for he could already foresee the outcome of his words.

"Big changes never come from diplomacy and half agreements."

Paradise Lost

He began in his raspy voice, "I tried you know, to just talk... But no one wanted to listen!

I had to prove that my way was better, I had to show the world what it was missing. Some of you here today remember that time, while others may sit confused."

He was right, all the old-timers knew exactly what he was talking about however anyone who believed in his "great lie" theory was at a loss.

"And I am afraid that that confusion is because of me..." mumbles started to rumble all around Kaustos. "I knew this day would come, the day when I would have to explain your salvation, explain it through my past sins." Kaustos paused and bit his lip, making tears fill his cold eyes.

"The Great Lie... was in fact, The Great Truth."

It took a few seconds to process but when it did an astonished crowed burst into a frenzy of noise and emotion.

The older ones all began shouting in rage and anger. The young ones however all looked shell shocked, standing in somewhat disbelief at the clarity that they were just given. Willows mind fallowed suite, she was in absolute shock.

Phillip on the other hand was screaming like a made man. However it wasn't rage that ignited his spirit but more a dimwitted sense of 'Everyone's screaming...I like screaming too... I'm going to scream now!'
Willow turned to him and smacked his head. "Shut-up so we can hear what he has to say next!"

Shiloh Callaghan

"Ouch! Why don't you smack everyone else's head!" complained Phillip. "I bet if Collin didn't run home to dream, you wouldn't have smacked him!"

"And I bet if you could use your mouth to eat, I would never have to hear you speak again!" fired back Willow. She was more hostile than normal. The "great lie" gave her a hiding place for her anger and frustration at the world around her. A history of Miracles and creation which never showed its face deserved some form of revenge; it deserved her lack of belief. 'But now what?' She thought to herself.

The crowd slowly began to calm down, Kaustos couldn't have been more pleased with the outcry and confusion that he just caused. Like a game of chess in his head, he moved his queen into position.

Soon the crowd silenced and allowed him to continue.

"I am truly sorry for misleading you. But to save our people it needed to be done, after all, who would have listened to the voice of a villain? No one… but a freedom fighter? That is someone people will listen to, so that's who I became."

"Why?" asked Solemn The Mayor, currying favor from the crowed. "Why now? Why not tell us immediately after the world dropped from under our noses that our people are still alive down there? For what possible purpose have you made us suffer for so long?!" He exclaimed.
Kaustos the thespian he was, now bowed his head in shame and answered a question the he had instructed Solemn to

86

ask. "From the information I was given, timing was important, timing was everything."

"What do you mean 'from the information I was given'?" asked the Major, "Given to you by whom?"

Kaustos looked into the crowed. His eyes slowly scanned back and forth until they rested on a spot near the edge of the world.

He lifted his finger and pointed, "I was told by YOU, The Visitor!"

Shiloh Callaghan

ACT4 SCENE4: Peek-a-boo

Everyone old and young alike turned their attention to a sparkling image near the Cliffside, to YOU.

A Look of shock quickly spread threw the crowed. Thanks to Kaustos, YOUR once shy shimmer which was only visible to some, now shone as brighlyt as the sun. (Rhyming unintentional)

A high pitch scream from the girl standing in front of YOU sent panic through the already excited crowed.

Older ones are gathering all around YOU now.

Look to YOUR left, that elderly man wants to speak to you,

"Who made YOU? Was it that fiend Kaustos? How in the world did YOU survive The Flaksen!?"

Go ahead and respond if YOU like, but I'm afraid it won't do much good. He won't be able to hear YOU, none of them can.

Philip gave Willow a look of 'ummmm.' then he made the noise "umm…. Before Collin left he said THAT THING was just a dream after all. So why can we see IT? Willow?"

She looked almost as confused. But with her personality Willow needed to say something definitive, or at least as definitive as a clueless person could, "He was right the first time, it wasn't a dream." Thinking some more she continued, "Before he told you THAT THING helped free him and Kaustos, right?"

"Yes."

"Well, what if it's true?"

"But the shackles" answered Philip, "they both still have them on, It can't be true!"

Willow looked up toward Kaustos with an untrusting eye. "What has The Professor always taught us about him?"

"That he used to be a male cheerleader." Philip replied, giggling at the thought.

"No! Well...yes he has always taught us that, but the other thing."

"Oh! That he lies."

"Yes" Willow replied as she began walking back towards the town.

Philip began to trot behind her, although unaware of their destination, "So where are we going?"

"To see Collin."

Philip slowed down, "What for? All the action is here!?"

Shiloh Callaghan

"Because if Collin was freed, he may be able to free us." She answered as her feet began to quicken in their stride. Phillip looked at YOU and then Kaustos with a bit of disappointment, "Hold on Willow! I'm coming!"

The two ran out of the crowed with hope on their faces, feeling that freedom could be a short distance away. For a theory that took Willow a whole minute to create, it wasn't bad. Although it was false. Collin was not freed; in fact he was more trapped than he had ever been before. But we will get to that part of the story later. I think you should focus your mind on the present situation. Try and look past all of the crazy-eyed spectators which are staring at YOU. Do YOU see Kaustos? He is about to speak.

"It isn't here to cause you any harm... And I didn't make it!" (speaking of YOU)

"How can we be sure!?" interrupted an angry old man from the crowed.

"Because it would be impossible!" replied Kaustos rather aggressively. "We all were shackled while my Flaksen were still alive. Only after they destroyed EVERYTHING created did they themselves disappear!" he roared. A few huffs of anger later Kaustos restored his composure, After all he still needed to be perceived as good, "What I meant is, I was a Villainous man before, but only a man, even I couldn't break through these shackles." He stretched out his hand towards YOU "I didn't create IT. But I do know IT'S harmless, I am sure of it."

Paradise Lost

Solemn stepped towards Kaustos, "How can you be so sure?"

"Because, it helped me solve the ancient puzzle.... It helped me translate The Tower."

The crowed gasped.

"When?" asked solemn.

"Just before the shackles appeared." replied Kaustos. "1,000 years go. I know there are differing opinions why I didn't stop The Flaksen from "destroying the world." Some have insinuated I wanted the destruction. Others say it was a mix of ignorance and negligence, then others still, such as Professor Stone, portray me as a distracted little girl chasing butterflies who was too arrogant to realize the plight of the world around me!"

"Then what really happened!?" asked the mayor while continuing to gawk at YOU.

"I was studying The Tower when THAT THING just appeared. At first I thought IT was some-ones creation, so I ordered a Flaksen to get rid of it. But the Flaksen couldn't, its teeth just flew straight through YOU, didn't they?" asked Kaustos with his annoyed face snubbing YOU.

"However soon after, IT showed me why IT came... IT helped me decode the secrets that have puzzled our people since the beginning of time.

Shiloh Callaghan

"What are they?!" asked the Mayor. The audience suddenly shifted there attention back onto Kaustos, as if YOU are not even there.

"They are Prophecies... a series of predictions about the future. You asked me why I waited so long to tell you all about this?"

"Yes" replied the Mayor, "What makes this moment so special?"

(A voice from Behind YOU) "I do!"

Paradise Lost

ACT4 SCENE5: The awakening… or not

"Wake him up."

"How? We tried everything, nothing seems to work!"

"Try and push him off the bed!"

"What!?"

"Don't be such a pussy-foot! Just do it!"

"But what if he has powers?! I don't want to startle him, he could accidentally blow my head up or something like that!"

"Don't be ridiculous!"

"If I am being ridiculous than why won't you do it?"

"You are both being ridiculous." a voice appeared from behind, frightening Willow and Phillip.

"Professor!" scolded Willow "Why are you sneaking about behind us?!"

"I am not sneaking" answered the professor, slightly insulted by the insinuation, "I'm just light on my feet. Besides I believe we are here for the same reason, to awaken sleeping beauty over there."

Shiloh Callaghan

"Well nothing seems to work!" said Phillip.

"That's because Collin isn't in a normal state of sleep." replied The Professor. "Something very powerful has sedated our friend. Which means we need something equally as powerful to awaken him."

"Like what?" asked Willow

"THE VISITOR, IT can help us."

"The what?"

"That THING you saw down by the Cliffside. I don't know what you think IT is, but you're wrong, of this I can assure you. Trust me, IT will help us to free Collin."

"Free him?" jumped in Philip "We thought he already was free."

"I'm afraid not." replied Professor Stone, "However he did see someone get set free."

"Well, call IT whatever you want" blurted out Willow, unaware of the important truth that The Professor had just spoke, "Let's just bring IT here to free Collin!"

Professor Stone: "We don't have to go to IT, IT will come to us. And soon."

"So what should we do now?" asked Philip

"Hopscotch?"

Paradise Lost

"Hopscotch?" interrupted Willow, with another scolding tone. "Don't you understand Professor, our world can soon be saved! My mother, my father are alive and you want to play hopscotch? This isn't some play to amuse you, old man!"

"But it is my child!" Quickly spoke the professor with his own words of conviction. "It is! I am sorry to say… but this whole ordeal with the balloon on a string… the idea of your parents still being alive, it's all a play…just not one for my amusement."

The last thing Willow wanted was an explanation of those words, however she couldn't help but ask for one. "What are you talking about?"

"Haven't you been listening? Collin was telling the truth about his trip to the prison, he just wasn't freed as he assumed. Kaustos on the other hand was, if you remember, that is what Collin saw. Ever since then, that villain has created a whole mess of false hope, toying around with the rest of the world as he pleases."

"Toying around!" shouted Willow in denial. "Isn't Kaustos supposed to be some super-evil person? We should see more destruction, not happiness and hope! You don't make any sense Professor!"

Stone could see how she would feel that way. She wasn't used to dealing with such devious tactics.

"I know it doesn't sound believable but this is what Kaustos does, he prides himself on manipulating people's

Shiloh Callaghan

beliefs. This is the destruction he enjoys above all else, not that of buildings and people, but that of the soul."

"My parents are alive!" she screamed "You horrible insensitive man!"

Willow's eyes began to burst into tears. Professor Stone gave her a moment for composure before speaking his next words.

"I want your parents to be alive Willow," he spoke gingerly, "I want it more than anything. You have no idea how often I dreamt the rest of the world was somehow floating below our own.

Why do you think I study, I obsess over The Tower every day? It's the only mystery left in our world. And since we have no hope, that makes it the only possible one. Willow, I have been searching for something, anything to know what to do next but the answer has always been out of my reach." The Professor pointed towards The Tower, "Then today of all days, came the missing piece to it's puzzle. I finally discovered how to read its engravings. It's a story Willow, one which leads up to this very moment in time. Your parents, the rest that fell off this earth, I am sorry but…"

"I DON'T BELIEVE YOU!" screamed Willow. "My parents are alive!" She stormed quickly past the Professor and out of the dormitory.

Paradise Lost

Philip was going to run after her until The Professor stopped him. "It's useless to try and catch her Philip, just let her go."

"Why, was something about Willow written on The Tower?" he asked, "Was she prophesied to run out of here and accomplish something important?"

"No, unfortunately you're just too big to chase her down, I thought I would save you the embarrassment" replied The Professor "Besides, now what is important is Collin. We must wait here until we can wake him up. Until after Dante rises."

ACT4 SCENE6: Dante's Accent

Everyone watched in amazement as a man once considered lost into the fog below not only ascended out of it, but flew into the air above it. Like stars shinning brightly from below, Dante looked down on all those hopeful eyes thinking only one thing, "Idiots!"

The reason for such a rude thought could be seen in the left hand of the man standing at the center of it all. Kaustos index finger moved slowly around and around as he controlled the image of an already dead Dante.

Sadly, just like Lancer, this young professor was a shell of a real person, no free will, no thinking or feeling. Simply another window for Kaustos mind to peek through as he manipulated the masses around him.

The cheers of amazement kept filling the air when Dante gracefully landed next to Kaustos and Solemn The Mayor.

Stretching out his unshackled hands towards Kaustos, he declared "Our hero!"

This crowd, like so many others in history was easily swayed. A man once so evil that a name was created for him to define his wickedness was now being looked upon as a Savior!

With one simple motion of his naked hands, Dante quieted the crowd.

Paradise Lost

"I have waited for this day. The time when I could show you to a better world, one with no suffering or pain... one that holds miracles which I once considered only as fantasy." Dante looked towards Kaustos "You lied to me about the power within us... But I can understand why he did it. The idea of The Great Lie gave me the strength and passion of a mega-hero, so I could risk my life in the face of so much opposition. A loving truth would never have worked. Your lie made me believe sir! So thank you!"

(You may ask yourself, "Did I just hear the word mega-hero?" well, yes, you did. Before the real Dante was killed, he was best described as a cocky-nerd-jerk-looser-self assuming-prideful weasel. Anyway, Kaustos knew that, thus the expression "mega-hero". Now back to the story!)

Dante again turned his attention towards the crowed which surprisingly was now lacking YOU.

"Who misses seeing these!?" he asked, showing off his pearly white teeth with a big smile.

A roar of laughter came from the older ones in the crowed.

"And if you are as young as I am, trust me, food tastes so much better through the mouth than through the nose," Dante fallowed that little gem of insight with his well-known snorting laugh. "Anyway, I can see a book-full of questions on all of your faces, so please allow me to knock a few of them out of the window of your minds. First, my freedom. What's up with that?! Hahaha! Well, it wasn't until recently that the "shackles" came off. And as much as I hate to admit it, I owe, No, let me correct that, WE owe our freedom not only to Kaustos but also to Professor Stone!"

The Professor although a little nutty was well liked in the world, so naturally an applause of support came from all around.

"Where is that old coot?" asked Dante with a grin "Oh, no matter I am sure he is listening somewhere. Now it's no secret me and Stone haven't always seen eye to eye, especially when I led my incredibly successful mission down into the unknown. I believe Stone called us 'the suicide squad'... whatever!" Dante laughed again, even sounding more arrogant than before. He then proceeded to mock The Professor just for the sake of doing it "Oh look at me, I'm Professor Stone, watch me put my finger in my butt and sing like a girl!"

The crowed didn't exactly know how to respond to that, it was a very weird statement. However it did show that Kaustos spent enough quality time with Dante to really understand how much he resented Professor Stone.

"Hahaha! Just a little joke between friendly rivals. Any-who, once we got down into the world below and saw the beauty and variety of a place built upon love, it slowly lead to our first dreams. After that happened, we decided that Stones freedom-through-dreams theory couldn't hurt anything, so we tried it. It took a longtime and we just about gave-up on believing it would work until one very special day. Little Cindy Parker woke up with her shackles off! We all went bananas with a capital B-A-N-A-N-A-S! The first thing she did was to reach out, grab me by my hands and say 'leader... friend... hero... be free!'" At this point Dante began to cry. You may think that Kaustos is exaggerating his interpretation, but trust me, he wasn't.

"Together we freed others. And I am happy to say now they are building up their energy to help free all of you as well! Why am I still talking about it, let me just show you!"

The small world in the sky nearly shook from the excitement caused by Dante's statement.

"In honor of Professor Stone, how about I re-make one of his old creations to get you all down there a bit easier!"

Dante stretched out his hands. The young generation in the audience all rushed to the front to look at what he was doing, they never saw a creation before, in-fact most of them didn't even believe in super-powers until 30 minutes ago.

They watched in amazement as Blue energy began to flow between Dante's fingers and then his hands. "Ooooh's and Ahhhs" followed as the energy rested all around Dante until he opened his mouth.

"Slide!"

And poof! A Slide made out of clouds appeared at the edge of the world (yes, a slide made of clouds). Probably not the best first creation to see, but it did the job.

Like happy little children the older ones rushed towards it. Without a second thought they all jumped down the slide, laughing and giggling as they went. The younger ones looked just as excited, but none went down the slide.

"I know you may be nervous about jumping!" assured Dante as he once again took flight. "I don't expect your faith to be as courageous as mine was! But believe your eyes, you can see me flying. And listen to your ears, the old ones are still laughing. There is nothing to be afraid of!"

Then landing near a young girl, Dante took her by the hand. "Everything will be okay."

She looked around at all of her friends. They were all smiling in excitement.

Shiloh Callaghan

Act 5

Fifth Law: Combining creations with element is allowed, yet do so with the utmost caution. This is were ultimate power lies

Paradise Lost

ACT5 SCENE1: Introduction

Willow:

"What are YOU doing on this road? What are YOU doing here at all! YOU don't frighten me YOU know, with the way YOU just stand there and watch like some weirdo in a tree! Is that what YOU are?

Shake your head no (continue reading)

Shake your head yes (please go to The Table of Possible Context)

So YOU can understand me? Then where are YOU from?

Are YOU something Collin made in his dream?
(You shake your head no)

Are YOU this "Visitor" then?
(You nod your head yes)

So what have YOU seen in my world?! What have YOU observed? My parents, they went down Dante's rope, are they still alive? Can I join them?

Perfect, YOU have the power to span between worlds but when it comes to communication, YOU can only answer yes or no to half of my questions...

Shiloh Callaghan

Do YOU enjoy the pain and suffering of my world?
No (continue reading)

Yes (please go to The Table of Possible Context)

Well, I don't believe YOU!

(Willow storms away toward the worlds end.)

<u>ACT5 SCENE2: Awakening</u>

The Professor and the two boys are just inside. They are waiting for you. I know, this old and dark building looks awfully depressing but it was the only place big enough to house all the orphans. It's sad that the generations after The War have such a short life. Most, like Collin and Philip's parents die in their late 20's leaving a slew of offspring to be unattended.

The boys live on the second floor, that's were YOU will find them. YOU better hurry, I'm depending on YOU.

"This is tiring, Professor, do I really have to keep going?"

"Yes! Jump! Jump!"

"Are you sure me jumping will help this 'VISITOR' to come quicker?" huffed out Philip.

"Well, you are creating a small seismic disturbance, but honestly I just wanted you to exercise." Replied the professor with a rather serious tone.

"You've got to be kidding me!"

Professor Stone: "Look!"

Both their eyes followed his finger until they rested on YOU. "Maybe your jumping did work!" Exclaimed Stone "Now let's get these shackles off!"

Shiloh Callaghan

He walked over to YOU and called for Philip to do the same.

"We both need to touch THE VISITOR at the same time in order for me to be set free. So come on with it, we don't have all day."

"You?" asked Phillip, rather confused. "I thought we would both be freed?"

"Well, not exactly. When Kaustos quoted the prophecy to Collin, he left out a key part."

"Which is?" asked Philip.

"Kaustos said the following recipe was needed, 'Two who can see, one who can dream and the other who believes, if both touch the unseen, all will be set free.' Rather poetic and slightly confusing, just like the writing on The Tower. However the real prophecy states this as the recipe for our freedom, 'Two who can see, one who can dream and the other who believes. If both touch the unseen, *the one who dream will be set free.*'"

Philip processed that as best as he could. Finally when the last synopsis was made, he said "Well, that's unfair! Why can't both be set free?!"

Professor Stone couldn't help but laugh. In the midst of all that was going on, Philip was concerned about The Towers justice.

Paradise Lost

108

"I'm afraid i don't know the answer my friend, perhaps The Towers creator honors the old. But lets get back to it, shall we?" continued The Professor as he ruffled his fingers in Philips hair, "I can dream. And thanks to Kaustos, you can see the unseen, which allows you to believe, right?"

Philip again tried his best to process what was said. All of those large rhyming words kicked around in his head until they finally landed on the 'I don't understand' square of the brain. However, that fact didn't stop an affirming "yes!" to bellow out from within.

With guidance from Professor Stone, Philip then walked towards you rather humbly. He stretched his arm out and gave a smile, "I am going to help set our people free."

"Yes, you will my boy."

They both touched YOUR hand. Can YOU feel it, that cold rusty steel resting upon your flesh?

CLINK! CLINK! CLINK! THUMP! THUMP! THUMP!

The Professor didn't hesitate to next set Philip free (followed by 3 more CLINK! then THUMPING sounds).

Professor Stone: "Open your eyes, son."

Philip's tightly shut eyelids opened to a smiling old man, one without a mask. He looked down at his own free hands. Wiggling his fingers and then touching his mouth, Philip struggled for breath. A joy which before he could never imagine now swarmed inside of him. Gazing up towards

Shiloh Callaghan

YOU he grinned from ear to ear. Can YOU see how happy he is?

"Thank you! Thank you!"

Look over at The Professor. See how still he stands. As if stitching this memory into his soul.

"Freedom!" he said.

Philip watched on as Professor Stone waved his hand, causing Collins shackles to fall to the ground. He again waved his hand and as if magic, a small pill appeared in it. "Now stick this in your friend's mouth and say the word, 'awaken.' By your power Philip, your friend will rise."

Philip did as he was told and then stood back and waited. And waited.

"Maybe I didn't do it right Professor?"

"Just wait."

It wasn't more than a moment afterwards that a gasp came out of Collins' unmasked mouth.

As he looked up at Professor Stone and Phillips unshackled hands and mouths, he also smiled, "I'm dreaming again!"

"No, you're not stupid!" quickly replied Collins' portly friend.

Paradise Lost

"Those old people lied to you!" He continued excitedly "Me and The Professor just saved you from some sleeping pill of death! Look at my mouth Collin, don't I look awesome!"

If Collin thought he was confused before, now he felt crazy.

Professor Stone went over to ease his student. "All will be explained but now I need to get you two ready."

"For what?" replied Philip.

"According to The Tower, WAR."

Shiloh Callaghan

ACT5 SCENE3: The bad guys!

Arriving at the end of the world, Willow found a former festive and exciting place, quit empty and void.

"Everyone must already have gone down," thought Willow as she stared at the bizarre slide dropping into the fog below.

She approached the cliff. By now reason was catching up with her and that former urge to jump was lacking its luster. All the things that The Professor had said, along with your own personal insights had cracked an opening through Willows blinding emotions.

She sat a healthy distance from the edge and gazed out into the fog, contemplating her next move.

"The girl's apprehensive" said Solemn to Kaustos as they watched Willow from a distance. "But she is of no importance I assume?"

"She wasn't mentioned as doing anything on The Tower." replied Koustos "But that doesn't mean she isn't important. Remember along with the rest of us she was still mentioned in the future battle. If something like, I don't know, pushing her off the cliff was to happen. The Towers future may not come to pass."

Looking down with a sharp pain of discontent, Solemn replied "Which is the same reason why I still need to wear these blasted shackles!"

Paradise Lost

"Yes." Responded Kaustos firmly "It's what The Tower has shown, we cannot risk any alteration."

"But when the moment is right, you will free me." stated The mayor, although his tone seemed to be asking more than stating.

"What's that?" quickly replied Kaustos in an authoritative way.

"Nothing. Just as you said, I cannot be free until the murder" stuttered out Solemn, "That's what you said before... you said that's what was written on The TOWER. Then you will free me after, right?"

Kaustos stared Solemn down until he just about melted in his boots. "My dear cousin" he spoke gingerly, "are you questioning my loyalty? How unwise." Creeping a little closer he continued "Maybe before I was freed, or before I killed all our comrades. Maybe even before WE tricked everyone to throw themselves off the worlds end, but not now cousin, do you understand? I am your only hope, I AM your God, and one should not question his God."

Trying his best to gulp down his fear The mayor replied, "It was a moment of impatience and nothing more."

"That's good." replied Kaustos with a short smile, "That's really good. Because everything we have done thus far could crumble unless we stay on course, unless we keep hope."

"Of course, of course."

Shiloh Callaghan

"Then what should you be thinking of next?"

"The boy, the fat one"

"And are you ready?"

"To kill him? Yes."

"Mmm." Huffed Kaustos as he looked back to the edge of the world, "The girl is gone."

"She couldn't have gone down, could she have?"

ACT5 SCENE4: Portal

Willow came crashing down from the ceiling of the boy's dormitory, landing butt-first in the middle of Collin, The Professor and Philip.

"Oh, sorry my dear girl!" exclaimed The Professor, "Philip was in charge of creating a cushion for you!"

"... I must have forgot." answered Philip with a mischievous grin.

"I bet you did!" Willow angrily protested as Collin helped her up.

She was about to greet Philip with a stiff punch to his metal plated mouth, when she saw that there was no metal plate! Then looking down at Collin's helping hands she couldn't believe her eyes.

"You are free!" Willow looked around. "You all are!"

As she continued to scan the room, her eyes rested upon YOU.

"So, it's true, my parents, they are..." the sad look on her face finished the sentence that her mouth could not.

Professor Stone went over to Willow. He rested his hands on top of her small rusted shackles.

Shiloh Callaghan

"I'm truly sorry my child, I can do nothing for your parents. Holding her mitts tight, The Professor spoke the words that Willow always and yet never wanted to hear, "Be free."

Immediately the girls shackles slipped off and thudded to the ground.

Still riddled with grief she looked up at Professor Stone, "How can I ever be free?"

At that moment Collin knew Philip wouldn't be able to stop himself from saying something incredibly insensitive like "look at your hands, you are free stupid!" so with a wiggle of his fingers and a whisper of breath, a small piece of tape strapped across his friends mouth. For a moment Philip gave Collin a scowl until his realized what Willow actually meant. Ripping off the tape he then smiled at Collin, relieved that he was now safe from the girls biting revenge.

In the meantime, Professor Stone was thinking long and hard before he spoke any further.

"To say that life has been unkind to you, all of you, wouldn't even began to dignify our suffering. But Willow, I must ask something of you. Whatever pain you are feeling, whatever anger you have toward those who lied to you, I need you to bottle them all up. I'm not asking you to let them go, but hold on to them and save them for another day. Can you do that for us?"

"Why?"

Paradise Lost

"Because for all of us to stay alive, we need your strength, your passion, my child! But we need it tempered with love, no other emotion will do."

Willow looked first at Collin. Then Philip, The Professor and finally YOU.

"But how can I? Love is the one thing I am missing."

Professor Stone gently slid his hand over Willow's eyelashes, "Close your eyes."

As she complied, he spoke these words

"Think of your mom and dad. In your mind recreate their faces. Can you see them?"

Willow nodded.

"Good. Now try and think of a happy memory of your mom, of your dad. Do you have one? (Again a nod) Remove their shackles child, can you see them smiling? Try and feel their love as they look at you with innocence wrapped around their faces. You are their baby girl, their everything."

The Professor stretched out Willows hand, "Now tell them hello my child... go on, say it."

Willows fingers began to flicker and then spark as she opened her mouth. "Mom, dad, I miss you. I miss you both so much!"

Shiloh Callaghan

Now YOU. Look in front of the girl. Can YOU see the slight mist appearing? The spark of energy from her fingers flying and skipping in the haze? Look closely in the mist, look at the two faces. That's Willows mom. That's her dad.
"I'm going to show you something" spoke The Professor. "It's not real, but it is a memory, one that will allow you to see the love that's still inside." He lifted his hands away from her face.

Her eyes opened to happiness, love and disbelief. Like figurines they both stood there smiling down on her.

"Mom, Dad?"

(No reply)

"They cannot speak unless you make them."

The mom's mouth opened "Willow?"

"That is her voice!" She walked towards them, thinking of something for her father to say.

"Hello, Wet-Willy. You look so pretty without that ugly mask on!"

Again Collin quickly strapped tape across Philips mouth.

"I miss you both so much!"

"We miss you too!" They both spoke.

Paradise Lost

Willow was at the height of ecstasy when a haunting voice suddenly appeared from behind, "It's a shame they are both dead, little girl!" She turned around. It was Kaustos!
Collin and Philip were shocked and looked to The Professor for direction.

Willow on the other hand didn't shift her eyes to anyone, not even for a second. Her hands are glowing with a fiery red sheen, can YOU see them?

Sparks flared as her eyes became black as coal. She then shouted out the one word that had been weighing on the tip of her tongue.

"DIE!"

Flames burst out from her fingertips, heading straight towards the villain, engulfing him in the inferno.

Willow stood and watched, again not looking away for a second. He gave a few twists and turns before collapsing to the ground. All watched on with a look of disgust as he lay motionless, still burning away into nothing.

Finally when Willows rage had subsided, she felt a grip of shame inside of herself, she no longer wanted to see the distraction that was left in her path. Her eyes turned back towards her parents, hoping to see their smiles once again.

But unfortunately the smiles were gone. In fact the image of both her parents had all but vanished into the mist in which it was created.

Shiloh Callaghan

"No!" she screamed. "What's happening? Professor help me make them come back!"

"I can't" he replied, standing by what was left of Kaustos body. "What have I always taught you? All of you?" The Professor looked to the boys as well. "Love creates, pride destroys."

He slowly waved his hand over the imitation-Kaustos which he had created, vanishing it into thin air.

"That feeling you have, Willow, the sickening one in the pit of your stomach that took root as soon as you saw Kaustos image burn, remember it. That's where revenge and pride lead my child. But the memory of your parents, that's where love leads. Okay?" The Professor smiled. "We create with love."

"Professor?"

"Yes, my child?"

"I'm ready."

Paradise Lost

ACT5 SCENE5: So here is the plan

"So here is the plan" spoke Professor Stone with excitement. "The writing on The Tower is clear, we must re-shackle Kaustos. Once that prophecy is fulfilled, I believe the symbols on The Towers walls will change, giving us new directions, new possible futures from there.

"Sounds great!" exclaimed Philip, eating a mouthful of cloud-candy which he had recently created.

Collin however didn't share in his friend's enthusiasm, or candy for that matter. "But if Kaustos read the prophecy Professor, why would he allow himself to be recaptured? Why would he allow any of us to even still be alive? It just doesn't make sense."

"Well, YOU can answer that question better than I could, can't YOU?"

All eyes turned towards YOU.

"Do YOU want to tell them or do I have to?

So you want to give me the honor, I humbly except."

In true Professor Stone fashion, he quickly created a miniature version of The Tower (about waist high) to demonstrate what he believed to be true. "Gather around children... YOU too my strange looking invisi-friend. Here is The Tower with all its symbols. Now let me show you what happened when me and our invisi-friend looked at it."

Shiloh Callaghan

The Professor wiggled his fingers to create a small figurine of himself and YOU.

"Professor?"

"Yes Collin?"

Looking at the representation that Stone had made of himself, Collin replied "You're not even close to being that good looking."

"What do you mean; it's a mirror image of myself!"

The three children looked at each other with a smile.

"Anyway as you can see, I stuck my face into the back of his so as to see the writing on the wall and..."

"Oh gross!!!!!!!" interrupted the children

Willow: "That just looks wrong Professor!"

Phillip: "You molested it!"

"Oh, come come now! I am sure IT didn't feel in anyway violated, did YOU?"

Nod no (continue reading)

Nod yes (please go to The Table of Possible Context)

Paradise Lost

"See there! No problem. Now back to what I was saying. When my eyes merged with those of The Visitors eyes, look what happens to the symbols."

They watched-on as the face of The Tower began to change. All the square blocks with their own unique symbol began to reshuffle into new places, finally creating a somewhat uniform look.

"When this happened, I could read into our past, our present and even our future."

"Well, what future did you see?" asked Collin

The Professors face weighed down as he replied. "One too horrible to mention."

Collin: "How is that even possible? Mostly everyone is already dead!"

"But we aren't. And if that future were to come to pass... let's just say it can't come to pass."

Collin, Philip and Willow were all curious of what that meant, but none dare ask.

After clearing his throat The Professor continued "The moment I saw that future, my mind could only wish, plead and beg for a different one. And that's when it happened."

Philip: "What?"

Shiloh Callaghan

The symbols that explained the future, they began to glow, then rearrange! The outcome was awesome!!! Based off of my desire, it told of another possible future, one that if the prophecy was obeyed, will grant us life."

"But not a hope of granting anyone fallen, life?" asked Willow.

"The Tower can only show you what is in the realm of possibility my child. Whatever damage Kaustos had already done to this world, can not be changed. Sadly, sometimes the past is too broken to entirely fix the future my dear." The Professor paused in a moment of reflection. "However, Kaustos allowed us to live, even allowing me to change the future that was set. This troubles me deeply. Somehow our lives, even this battle we will have, benefit him."

"How?" asked Phillip

"Now that is the real question. And the answer is one that I do not know."

Paradise Lost

ACT5 SCENE6: Preparation for war

Kaustos: "The hardest part of a battle is not the fighting, but it is the perception and understanding of one's enemy."

"And what has The Tower helped us to understand about our enemy?"

"The children are being trained how to create Shackles of hands and tongues. And however temporary, they are being made especially for us. As we speak I can almost hear Stone's pathetic voice 'by harnessing your creative strength, you have the power to imprison these evil GODS!' It's almost amusing."

"When does The Tower say that the children will enter onto the battlefield?"

"You mean when will the fat one come? The one whose blood you need to free yourself? Remember what we talked about before! I'll tell you what is on The Tower when the time comes for you to know is right."

"Of course Kaustos, I am just anxious to join in the battle, I remember how... difficult Stone was during The War."

"Yet his fate will be the same!" Snapped Kaustos as he sucked in his teeth and spat out a loogie in disgust. "I've been preparing more than one creation for this little battle ever since I was freed. And I promise you, his blood will drip from my hand before the next sunrise!"

Shiloh Callaghan

Stretching out his hand Kaustos spoke the words to create a most sinister object, a weapon.

"This is what will be used to kill our prey." Opening Solemn's hand he placed it inside.

"First you the boy, then me, Stone. It took nearly half of my creative energy to forge this. Neither Stone nor the children would be able to make a creation to stop it before it's too late. "

Solemn smiled. "What now?"

"Now, we wait for the moon to bleed."

<u>ACT5 SCENE7: The Power of the already existed</u>

"So, I bet YOU are bored by now...Professor how much longer is this going to take, The Visitor told me IT is bored!" shouted Philip as his outstretched arms poured energy into a pair of shackles.

Stone was quick to respond, however in a much less humorous tone, "Unless you want Kaustos to break free from those in seconds only to create some diabolical creature to rip every appendage off of your body, you will keep infusing those shackles I made with power!" he huffed.

"What's an appendage?" question Philip to Collin.

"I think it's stuff that extends from your body" he replied "Arms, legs, fingers, toes and... you know... The other thing."

"NO! That's not what it means! No one is evil enough to create something that would rip that off, would they Professor?"

With a stoic look, Professor Stone answered "EVERY APPENDAGE."

"More power!!!!" screamed Philip, as his pelvis fearfully sunk inward.

The children kept working on the shackles when Stone went to the window and looked up at the night sky. "It's dark out there" he noticed with a slight irritation. Knowing that the battle was near he looked back at a melting candle which rested on the table. "Whoever wants to see something extraordinary, take a short break."

Immediately Willow stopped her work on the shackles and focused solely on The Professor. However it took the boys a few seconds to decide if whatever it was was actually worth the break. The word "Appendage" kept running through their minds.

"Don't worry boys, this won't take so long." reassured Stone, knowing what they were thinking.

Now feeling safer, they ran over to watch what was going to happen.

"I wish you would all have paid this much attention in class, when I actually taught you about creation." teased Stone.

"There were never visual aids in your class, Professor."

"That is true, Collin," he agreed "which may have led some to vandalize a certain bathroom with graffiti, am I right?"

A bit shame ridden, Collin gave no reply.

The Professor took the candle over to the window and raised it toward the sky, "Who remembers what would happen if i mix a natural element, such as fire, with something created?"
Everyone looked to the other to answer. No one did.

Paradise Lost

"Why did I even waste my time!" he huffed, "Just SEE so you can learn and maybe actually believe."

He pointed his finger up in the air towards the now floating candle. Slowly he aligned his index finger with the candle, and the planet closest the moon.

"Elements contain far more power than we can ever generate, even one as small as this flame." The Professor steadied his hand and simply said one word, "GO!"

The flame shot up, streaming through the air and all the way into the heavens. The Children watched as the small planet began to shine brighter and brighter. It looked as if the Professor was holding it, like some strange kite on a firry string. His students were amazed.

"Now watch the moon!"

Can YOU see it? YOU are just behind The Professor, I'm sure YOU can. See how the moon is beginning to reflect the fire that has ignited the planet?

When Stone saw the moon brightly reflecting the burning planet, he withdrew his finger and the string of fire quickly vanish.

Afterward he floated the candle back over to the desk on which it laid. It was almost a majestic moment until Willow scolded,

"You just killed a planet!"

Shiloh Callaghan

However the boys spoke the same five words, except with enthusiasm "You just killed a planet!"

The Professor chuckled "I didn't kill it. But it will shine all night, until the morning. Every year we used to burn it for the festival of lights."

At that point The Professor smiled as he reminisced about the beauty of the past. "Maybe you vaguely remember that story... Or perhaps you dismissed it only as a story. Anyway, to the present. You all know the plan. When the shackles are near completion you must bring them to the battlefield. I will need your help by then, so don't dilly dally!"

With a concerned face, Collin spoke up, "I know that's what The Tower says we will do Professor, but...what if we mess things up?"

"You won't" reassured Stone "I didn't give you any details of what will happen for a reason, it takes away choice, giving you only one path, the right one. Do you understand?"

"I do." replied Collin.

The Professor walked over to a wall and pressed his hand onto its cold concrete surface. There was a snapping sound that followed. Soon the outline of a doorway appeared in its fractures. CRACK! CRACK! CRACK! In the matter of seconds the concrete crumbled away, leaving a doorway framed in darkness.

Paradise Lost

"This Portal only goes one way, so don't forget the shackles when you come through."
"We won't" replied Collin.

Professor Stone then created a force-field around himself and bit them adieu.

"See you on the other side."

Paradise Lost

Act 6

Amendment of the First Law: Create with love. However, if one chooses to follow the unrighteous path, creating to kill, He shall be bonded forever, until the Sun no longer shines.

Shiloh Callaghan

ACT6 SCENE1: Reintroduction

Solemn:

Well, here we are again, from the beginning to the end.
I wish I could see the expression on YOUR face. Is it one of horror or one of happiness? Are YOU a person of pride and progress or a silly believer in love? If YOU are the latter, it must pain YOU deeply to know that YOU were the catalyst for all the deaths that took place here. All those lives, all that suffering yet YOUR care and concern did nothing to help! However if YOU are the former, a person of true wisdom and understanding then I can only imagine the joy you must feel.

I should be freed any hour now. I do hope you will enjoy the sound of it; that ever-so-amazing ringing of pain molesting YOUR ears when I secure my freedom with this blade.
If YOU want, I can make YOU a keep-sake of the boy. He would be easy enough to draw. That is, if YOU would miss him?

(explosions in the distance)

Ah! That's the sound I have been waiting for.

Be YOU friend or foe, we will see each other on the battlefield.

Paradise Lost

ACT6 SCENE2: The battle

The Professors body was flung into the air as soon as he appeared through the portal.

Bullets, bombs, and blades all scattered around and into him as he fumbled on and off the ground. Crashing and smashing into rocks and walls as he went. His force field already showed signs of wavering.

SMACK!

As he crashed into a stone embankment he tried to quickly create something to retaliate, but with another BOOM! BOOM! BOOM! Dropping on and around him, it seemed unlikely that that would happen anytime soon.

Much like in the war, Kaustos had little patience for things like mercy and chivalry. His plan was simple, nonstop death. And as more bombs dropped, it seemed to be working. Stone began to question if he had misread the prophecy or if he had change something that would cause his untimely demise. And as he again found himself a rag doll in the wind he worried more and more.

CRASH! Again he collided to the ground.

Stone barely had a chance to breathe before something immense grabbed a hold of him. It raised him high in the air. Everything was happening so fast and The Professor's mind raced to catch up to the present. "What in the world has a hold on me?!" He thought, unable to see his attacker.

Shiloh Callaghan

But YOU can see it, can't YOU?

I would personally describe it as mutated in-bread Ogre spit. It's large, beastly, slimy and worst yet, hungry.

Crunch! The Ugly freak began to bite down on Stone, trying to break through his already weakened force-field.

"AHHH! " He screamed... "Your breath stinks!"

Wiggling his fingers, The Professor quickly created what looked like a huge piece of peppermint candy, placing it directly in the center of the creature's mouth.

Hovering high and nearby, Kaustos watched on and was quick to catch Stones first creation of the battle. "It's a bomb!" he yelled, "Spit it out!" he commanded the colossal beast.

The monster loogied out the round peppermint striped cylinder along with Professor Stone, smashing them both to the ground. With his force-field finally gone, Stone lay dazed and covered in monster snot.

Coughing as he spoke, he blurted out, "It wasn't a bomb, it was honestly a mint!"

Unfortunately that bit of truth enraged Kaustos even more, "You are a twit, Stone!"

"Yes, but not as big of a twit as you think." remarked The Professor. He snapped his fingers to reanimate his force-field. However, this time it wasn't enclosed around his body, but that of Kaustos. Temporally this was as good as shackles, but Stone knew it wouldn't contain Kaustos for long.

Looking over at the ugly beast, he could see its link to Kaustos was now interrupted.

"You didn't have enough time to give it it's own spark, did you?" asked Stone.

Looking back at Kaustos for a reply all he could hear were muted obscenities.

"From dust you are, to dust you will return" spoke The Professor as he simply moved his finger across the neck of the beast.

THUD! number one: the head.

THUD! number two: everything else.

With the wind blowing off the world's edge, Stone created a strong enough force to dispatch of the creature and send it spiraling into the fog below.

Again, looking back at Kaustos, The Professor saw a spitting, shouting lunatic, gashing himself open with uncontrolled rage, all in an effort to break free.

He approached Kaustos slowly, sizing up his former colleague as a hunter would a lion in a cage. Now standing a few feet away from the already cracking barrier of good vs. evil, he spoke,

Shiloh Callaghan

"What a waste."

As Kaustos spewed venom back (literally), The Professor flung out one hand toward a boulder. He then created a portal underneath it. The exit-portal immediately appeared above Kaustos' head. Like a conductor of a symphony, Stone waved his other arm toward the force-field and snapped his fingers. Kaustos now found himself freed from bondage, however this time wearing a falling crag for a hat.

THUD!

It dropped too late. And in the blink of an eye, Kaustos vanished from under its shadow.

Instantly appearing behind The Professor, vengeance took its form in a raised dagger. However redemption took its form in a cream pie, smashing Kaustos square in his face.

The Professor bolted to the air with a slight laugh of arrogance, "Did you think I would actually sully my hands with your filthy blood, boy! Next time I'll be sure you are part of the ruse, maybe then you will know how to keep your face clean."

The words "Utter disrespect" could be defined in many ways. However for Kaustos, Stones actions were definition number one. Incensed to near blindness, he summoned more of his stored power.

Still hovering high above Kaustos, The Professor began to see a circle of energy emitting from his foe. Reds, blues, and greens all sparked violently as they swarmed around

138

the villain. Playfulness quickly vanished from Stone as he knew what was coming.

"So this is when it happens."

ACT6 SCENE3: BLAST!!!

Energy blazed out of Kaustos' outstretched fists and a solid beam of electric light rushed towards The Professor.

Can *YOU* see him now? With the pastel red sky in the backdrop, he is trying his best to avoid the blue energy that crackles toward him. But YOU know he cant escape it, don't *YOU*? It's obvious that no matter how many times he flips, spins, disappears or fights back, he will soon meet Kaustos wrath.

And with no time for a portal, or enough energy for a force-field, *YOU* see it happen.

"AHHHHHHH!"

Slowly lowering his fists, Kaustos again smiled with evil satisfaction.

"I guess you were right" he blurted out to a falling Professor, 'pride goes before a crash' after all."

THUD!

Walking over he bent down and picked up what was left of Stones severed arm. Immediately he ignited it, turning it to ash.

"No getting that back now."

Paradise Lost

And in a rare but habitual moment, Kaustos paused the battle to salute himself for shedding first blood.

Seconds later another and much bigger THUD landed behind Kaustos. Turning to The Professors, now planted into the ground, he gloated "Who's the boy now?!"

Lying in agony, Stone gave the most appropriate response for that situation,

"Your mamma!"

"Oh, come now, again with childish insults. You know where that just got you." replied Kaustos as he stepped on Stones opened wound.

Another scream of agony rang out loud in *YOUR* ears.

Professor Stone: "Don't be so proud of something we both READ and KNEW WOULD and HAD TO happen!"

"True, but we didn't know HOW it would happen. I personally enjoy the gritty aftereffects of a dismemberment-by-energy blast. And on top of the how, only one of us knows the WHY, isn't that right?" Leaning in, Kaustos continued with a raspy whisper, "For example, why haven't I killed you yet? Why will I allow the children to come through that silly portal of yours? And my personal favorite, why will I let you win?"

The Professor couldn't deny his ignorance to all of those questions. However there was one slight amendment he wished to add.

Shiloh Callaghan

"You left one important WHY out."

Kaustos immediately looked around in panic. The obvious slyness in Stones words meant that some sort of trickery was a-foot.

"Why is an evil genius such as yourself talking to me, a mere image of the handsome Professor Stone?" asked the body.

Kaustos instantly stomped the fake body into dust.

"Where are you old man?!"

Stone was hiding just beneath the clouds, resting on the bottom of the slide.

"This will take a lot of energy and concentration" he admitted with frustration as he prepared to make a prosthetic. He could hear Kaustos creating. And it wasn't long before he could hear what was served up. The sound of hungry vultures searching and scanning overhead rang all around The Professor. He knew care was needed if he wanted to preserve what was left of his self proclaimed "sensual physique" (After all, the prophecy may have promised him his life, but made no such assurances about keeping the rest of his limbs).

Can *YOU* hear them? The immense sound of all those disfigured and starved fledglings searching for the one and only food that they were programmed to eat?

Paradise Lost

"There must be thousands." Thought Stone as their squawking thundered through the sky.

He knew that it was only a matter of time before he was found. Rousing himself up, he prepared his next plan of attack, "Well, I better give the audience what they came to see."

Shiloh Callaghan

ACT6 SCENE4: Enter the children

The Professor quickly appeared on the ground.

In second a few vultures spotted him and they sounded the alarm, dinner had arrived. Like water circling the drain, a spiral of feathers formed overhead and came crashing down on top of him. As The Professor looked up, his face was covered in shock, anger and horror.

I'm sorry; at this point *YOUR* vision must be blurred. There are far too many creatures to see the ruckus that is underway. I'll try my best to explain.

Creating thousands of vultures which only are designed to eat one man comes at no cheap cost in terms of power. In contrast, creating a veil that covers another mans skin to look much like your own is rather cheap. And as in the game of chess one false move can quickly change the tide of a match, so too in a fight between good and evil. Especially when this particular part of the battle was not prophesied.

Now, enter the Children.

They all jumped through the portal holding small shields that had taken all but 2 seconds to create, (ergo it would take Kaustos 2 seconds to destroy). Nonetheless they were rather confident in their ignorance until the real Professor blasted the shields out of his students hands with a quick movement of the finger.

Paradise Lost

"Confidence in crap will get you killed!" He yelled, competing with the sound of feasting vultures.

"Very poetic!" replied Willow.

Collin nervously looked around, already shacking from the battle he had not yet fought.

"What are those things!?" he asked, looking over at a mountain of birds

"Some cursed creations that were designed and programmed to eat me."

"Well, why are they all over there?"

"They're trying to eat me of course!" He replied as if asked a stupid question. Continuing he spoke, "Now Kaustos energy is low, so as long as I am powering that veil, he won't be able to strip it off."

"WHAT?!" they all screamed in confusion.

"Kaustos! His has to kill off those pesky creatures on top of him, until then we are free!"

"So, Kaustos is in the middle of those things?" Asked Willow rather confused. I thought they were programmed to eat you?"

"Oh, try and keep up!" Stone screamed in frustration, "Now who has the shackles?"

Shiloh Callaghan

"I do." replied Philip.

"Good, you keep charging them, while we prepare for battle."

"Professor?"

"Yes, Willow?"

Looking over at the now shrinking pile of birds, she asked "Is it too late to kill him? He is weak, vulnerable. I don't care what the prophecy says Professor, killing Kaustos could only help!"

Stone immediately replied with unflinching conviction, "We are creators of good, love. We DON'T kill! Is that understood? (begrudgingly it was) Now Kaustos will free himself soon enough and when he..."

BOOM!

They all looked in the distance at a pillar of feathers dispersing over Kaustos head. Enraged, he came out firing. One hand after another.

Brimstone engulfed in flames flung over at the children.

Stone immediately raised up brick walls in front of the them (using a good amount of energy to do so).

CRASH!

Paradise Lost

The brimstone hit, causing explosions to happen all around, and sadly in Philips case, this caused one explosion within, (pooped pants).

"He's free! Let's move!" yelled The Professor. But as the fireballs kept coming it was absolutely obvious that fear had planted Collin, Willow and Philip behind the safety of their small walls.

"I thought the prophecy said **the children** would come to help?" thought The Professor as he observed an opposite truth.

Until this moment Stone was rather stingy with the energy he had been storing since his freedom. But if there was anytime to tap into it, now was it.

"Don't worry! It will stop soon!" He reassured the children, preparing for his counter strike.

In the meantime however, Kaustos was like a hose of death, never wavering from his assault. And since he knew that The Professors' battle code didn't include deadly force, he wasn't the least concerned when he saw an immense energy burst around his foe. In fact, he even seemed pleased,

"That's what I have been waiting for!" he mumbled.

Shiloh Callaghan

ACT6 SCENE5: Tiger-Counter-Strike!

As soon as their freshly created paws touched the ground, both tigers ran full-steam ahead into the line of fire. Deflecting and pulverizing through brimstone, it almost seemed that the more they were hit, the stronger they became.

Kaustos could tell immediately that these cats were created with a free-will of their own. He could see it in the wildness of their eyes. Although he was confident Stone didn't create them with the instinct to kill, accidents caused by "creations of defense" have happened in the past. And since whatever Kaustos threw at them only energized the power of their stride, he had no choice but to retreat with them in hot pursuit.

The Professor collapsed the walls in front of the children.

"It's safe now. Until he figures out what will stop our two new friends, he won't be back."

"Two new friends?" Unfortunately all six eyes were closed tight during their salvation, leaving them unaware of their new heroes.

"The Two Tig..."

"Professor!" yelled Willow as she ran to him with earnestness.

"Yes, my dear?"

Paradise Lost

"Your arm... it's gone!"

Collin and Philip also came to his aid.

"Why aren't you in pain?" asked Collin.

"Because I don't have to see Kaustos ugly face" jokingly replied The Professor as he recreated a prosthetic. "Don't worry, I'll be back to normal when I have enough power to create a proper replacement."

"No, you won't!" yelled Collin with a surprising amount of rage in his voice, "You said it yourself, a real prosthetic will drain power from you the rest of your life, it will take you twice as long to create things now!"

The Professor smiled, "So, you did pay attention in class." He looked at all of them. "I thank each of you for your concern, but now is the time to worry about the present, not the future. Philip, create yourself some new pants and finish charging those shackles."

"New pants?" asked Willow.

"Never mind that" replied The Professor as he motioned for the two tigers to return. "Let me introduce you to your saviors."

Feeling The Professors request, the two animals quickly returned from their hunt.

As they came trotting from afar, The Children looked with amazement.

Shiloh Callaghan

"Are those Tigers?" Asked Philip while pouring more energy into the shackles.

"Yes, let the myths come to life." Replied Stone pride-fully.

The two tigers made their way back and almost by instinct, nuzzled against The Professor with a pet-like affection.

The children looked on in envy.

"Can I touch them?" asked Willow.

"Sure, all of you can." replied The Professor with a smile. Watching the joy that the children had petting his creations gave Stone a remembrance of the past, a time when that type of joy had filled the earth.

"What are their names!?" asked Collin.

The Professor hadn't given them names yet. In fact, he thought it would be rather pointless, Kaustos will surely figure out a way to kill them before the night was over. However, he didn't have the heart to tell the children that.

"The one with the scar over its right eye... is named Scar" Stone replied, "and the one with the big paws is... Mu..Mufas..."

"Those are horrible names!" interrupted Willow.

"Yeah, maybe if they were lions, but not tigers!" chimed in Philip.

Paradise Lost

The Professor laughed, "Well, I'll leave the naming to you. But let's worry about that later, shall we?"

They all agreed.

Collin and Willow stayed with The Professor and The tigers, while Phillip was instructed to go to the small sliver of land in-between the old tree and the edge of the world to work on the shackles.

"It's the safest place" spoke The Professor to an apprehensive Philip. "Kaustos doesn't have enough energy to create a Portal to you now; the only way for him to get there is through us."

"Are you sure?"

"Its only 50 yards away. But ill tell you what, if you want you can take one of the tigers with you."

"Okay!" he replied without hesitation.

"Just don't sit on him, Professor Stone only made it with the power of one arm!" yelled Willow as Philip and the tiger walked away.

"Enough tomfoolery" spoke The Professor, "We'll need to create more than a tiger to stop Kaustos."

"Professor?"

"Yes Collin?"

Shiloh Callaghan

"To stop him from what?"

"I'm still not sure."

<u>ACT6 SCENE6: 10 minutes later</u>
(yes, it did take Phillip 10 minutes to walk only 50 yards)

Laying as flat as possible, Solemn clinched his dagger tight as he lay in wait . Cloaked in the tall grass around him, he hears Philip talking to the tiger in the distance,

"So can you talk? ... I guess not. Kind of like that weird invisible thing huh? Did you know I couldn't talk until I was like 4? Weird, right? Okay, so here we are. Time to get shackle-cooking!"

Solemn gingerly lifted up his head. no more than 5 yards away he could see Philip and a tiger approaching. "Just as Kaustos said" he thought. Laying back down, he waited for the opportune moment, for the time when he would hear the second roar.

Shiloh Callaghan

ACT6 SCENE7: A bucket of water

Willow and Collin rushed back and forth, collecting as many rocks as they could, dropping them in front of The Professor.

"Can't we just create something to do this?" complained Willow.

"It's a waste of Power! in battle every bit counts." answered The Professor as he tried his best to stack the stones one on top of the other. "More running, less talking!"

"I wish we had your job!" complained Willow as she ran by the Tiger. His big paws rested easy into the ground, staying as still as a statue, looking intently ahead, scanning for any sign of Kaustos.

"Kids today! No work ethic, huh tiger?" asked Collin, somewhat mocking The Professor as he dropped off his load.

"Don't expect an answer!" replied Stone as he overheard Collin.

But surprisingly the tiger gave one. Only its answer was to a different question, the one that sounded something like "When will the grotesquely ugly and evil uncle from Psycho-ville come over for dinner?" And as he stood up slowly, growling from deep within, the answer was "NOW."

Paradise Lost

"Quickly!" shouted The Professor. "The time is upon us!"

With it's claws extended and bolted into the ground, the tiger was ready to sprint towards danger. However Stone called it to stay, "He surely has an antidote for you by now my friend or he wouldn't have come back, let's just wait and see."

With the swagger and pace of a man who knows that he holds all the cards, Kaustos sauntered toward a pathetic looking wall made of stone.

Willow and Collin peeked through the cracks in the wall. They could see him coming from a distance with the old bucket used for the water well in hand.

"He must have come from the other side of the world." Whispered Collin.

The Professor: "With a bucket of water I presume?"

Willow: "How did you know?"

"Natural elements will win every time in a war. We chose defensive elements and now he has offensive ones."

Willow: "Well, I'm not afraid of a little water! And I'm sure Miss Tiger isn't either."

"First of all this is the boy tiger...

Willow: "How can you... oh!"

Shiloh Callaghan

...and secondly without this wall, that bucket of water could easily kill all of us 1000 times over, including our fury friend here."

Collin: "He is getting closer!"

Kaustos stopped a stone's throw from the wall (a long stone's throw).

"Well, have *YOU* been enjoying yourself so far."

"Your mamma!" replied The Professor

"I wasn't talking to you, you do-gooding freak! I was obliging The Visitor. Now where are YOU?... Ah! there YOU are! Why don't YOU come a little closer... let's chat a bit, shall we?"

Agree to go closer (keep reading)

Stay where you are (please go to The Table of Possible Context)

"I'm curious if YOU remember when we first meet, all those years ago? Come on, don't be so bashful, after all we are all here at this place, in this moment of time because of YOUR actions. YOU and YOUR pathetic sad world, YOU just couldn't help but visit ours could YOU? Are YOU enjoying YOUR tea? Coffee perhaps? Yes, I know far more about YOUR "earth" than YOU think. But YOU didn't come all the way here for me to talk about YOU and YOUR life. No, YOU came here to escape from YOU and

YOUR life. YOU came for a show. Well here is the grand finale!"

Kaustos dropped the bucket onto the ground and looked ahead towards the wall.

"Listen well Children, its time for a story!" he yelled as he motioned 3 drops of water up into the air. "Once upon a time, there was a big bad wolf!" barked out Kaustos. "And a few fat and stupid pigs who built houses. Sound familiar? Maybe your Professor taught this to you. I must admit, the beginning is quit good but the ending I could do without. All of that huffing and puffing, but that last fat piece of meat escapes!"

Snapping his fingers, the drops of water froze into tiny but sharp pieces of ice, then he motioned once more. "Now if I could write the ending, The wolf would huff!..."

SMACK! One drop of ice thundered into the wall.

Willow: "I'm scared Professor!"

"...Then he would puff!"

CRACK! Went another.

Professor: "We are safe, Philip will be done soon!"

"...And finally, he would blow the house down!"

Shiloh Callaghan

It was too fast for The Professor to see, maybe even for YOU as well. But both of yoU could hear the result of the third piece of ice.

It was a skull cracking smash that went through one of the tigers head.

"ROARRRRRRR!"

If YOU only had six eyes, for this is where the story becomes 3.

ACT6 SCENE8: Story 1 The Professor

"NO!" he screamed. The Professor quickly looked at the wall. There was one stone missing from its center.

"How?" he thought. His question was shortly answered however when another stone vanished before his very eyes.

"This is checkmate again, old man!" Yelled Kaustos as he took away another one of his creations.

The walled crumbled in front of its refugees. At this moment The Professor froze. He knew that this was it, the culmination of whatever Kaustos had devised was going to now come crashing down. They had lost and he knew it.

After all, the wall was prophesied to stand.

Shiloh Callaghan

ACT6 SCENE9: Story 2 Willow

A person who has lost almost everything, will do almost anything to keep what they have.

As Willow looked down at the panting Tiger, she immediately threw herself onto it.

"We need you! We need you!" she screamed. Pressing her hands over the bloody wound, she unwittingly surged all that her hands possessed into the upper left temple of its head.

"HEAL! PLEASE HEAL!" She screamed. The last bit of energy released itself from her body, collapsing Willow onto the beast.

ACT6 SCENE10: Story 3 Collin

Collin was bunkered with his back against the wall when the drops of ice hit. The first two he felt with a pounding pressure as the they shot into the real stones. The third one, however, was a far more fear inspiring experience. It just so happened that his eyes caught the very moment of penetration into The Tigers head.

"ROARRRRRRR!" The pain could be seen across its face. It seemed as if Collin was in a trance as he watched the agony. However a few seconds later he refocused towards the rest of the world after he heard another horrific roar. This one was from the second tiger.

It leaped into action, running towards danger, as it was created to do.

Everything was happening so fast. Collins eyes raced along with the approaching tiger until they skipped back towards the tree, towards a ghost that appeared in the wake of the tigers footsteps.

This man whom Collin was told had already been murdered by Kaustos, approached his best friend with death in hand. It was obvious now that Philip was the third little pig, and Solemn was the wolf. Collin could see his friend absorbed in completing his task, completely unaware of his own execution.

Shiloh Callaghan

The Mayor flung his arm up as quick as Collin could his. With equal speed and purpose their hands came crashing through the air. However only one reached its target.

With his hand still out, Collin froze in disbelief. And as with The Professor behind him, he was at a complete loss.

ACT6 SCENE11: Encore

"They're finally finished!" yelled Philip. He quickly came out from behind the tree and began to steam ahead towards the others when his body smacked into Solemn. It took one short glance at The Mayors desperate face, his arm projecting a dagger, and Philip became ravaged by dismay.

"SHIELD!" he yelled. His hands immediately dropped the shackles and grasped onto a new creation. After holding his breath and closing his eyes, he sank behind his shield and waited for the attack.

(sound of Stumbling) An attack which never came.

A few seconds passed and Philips' curiosity induced enough courage to peek out of his shell. There stood The Mayor staggering about with a gaping hole in his chest. His eyes were unfocused, searching, and looking, as if life would somehow lend him a hand.

YOU can see the look on Philip's face. It's completely void of his ordinary humor, isn't it? No witty one-liner was going to fly out of his mouth, not even a hint of sarcasm.

Death and blood can bridle the tongue of all.

A muttering came out of Solemn's mouth "Almost..free!"

Now zoom *YOUR* lens of sight out. GO ahead, stop when Kaustos, The Mayor and everyone in-between are in view.

Shiloh Callaghan

YOU got it?

Yes (please continue reading)

No (please go to The Table of Possible Context)

Good.

Solemn's gaze is focusing. His eyes and Kaustos' meet. Don't blink, for the moment is brief. But can YOU see it? The look of betrayal looming on the face of one, with a demented satisfaction beaming bright on that of the other? Solemn had served his purpose. And as he finally exhaled his last breath and collapsed to the ground, he died not as a man, but as a means to an end.

Philips eyes fallowed the pierced body that dropped before him. When he looked back up, he saw Collin still standing with his arm out and smoke lifting off of his fingertips.

"Collin!" yelled Philip over and over again as he ran towards him.

The Professor was finally roused out of his past memories by the prodding of a scare-faced tiger. He quickly looked around and feared the worst. Closest to him was Willow, laid out on the ground. However this didn't cause much alarm because the big pawed tiger was now healed and standing protectively by her side. Putting 2 and 2 together he knew Willow would be okay, she was just overdrawn.

The Professor yelled "Attack!" to the tigers, pointing the beasts toward Kaustos.

Paradise Lost

Phillip came running into sight. As The Professor saw the shield on his arm, he power-grabbed it and flung it at the bucket of water resting near his enemy. However it wasn't surprising that Kaustos had some form of a force-field around it, sending the shield flying as it bounced off.

"What has happened!?!?" Yelled The Professor. He watched Kaustos pick up a few drops of water for his pouncing challengers. They were approaching Kaustos fast, but it seemed pointless. Just a drop of water and the snap of his wrist would put an end to these animals.

Kaustos face seemed confused as they approached. But why the confusion, he's the bad guy, just kill em!!!

In a baffling move however, he chose a different approach. One shot hit each tiger in the paw, sending them fumbling and tumbling on the ground.

Scrolling back to The Professor, he had spent the last 30 seconds retrieving the Shackles, although not by his own feet rather with hands and tongue. He then tied them to his waist.

"Collin!" urged Philip "Snap out of it!"

"No time for that!" yelled Stone, throwing Collin to the safety of the ground.

(Still unaware of Collin's recent actions) The Professor told Philip, "For whatever reason, the boy is shell-shocked, just keep him safe!"

Shiloh Callaghan

Stone grabbed a few rocks and charged at Kaustos, knowing only one thing:

Unless his enemy still needed him, these would be the last steps he would ever take.

Paradise Lost

ACT6 SCENE12: The battle ends

The Professors stride gave a hint to his method of attack, All Or Nothing. Supercharged and screaming like a warlock, he pelted the first stone at the bucket of water. Kaustos quickly and easily power-grabbed it out of the way.

A sharp burst of frustration spat out of The Professor's mouth as he pushed forward, passing the two injured tigers to a patiently awaiting enemy. Releasing fire, mud, rocks, rubbie duckies, even a kitchen sink from his fingers as he neared Kaustos, Stone hoped for a distraction which would allow a chance for a final throw.

Kausots gestured wildly in defense at all that flew toward him. The Professor saw his moment and hurled his last stone into the air.

Sadly, however, it was met with defeat.

A piece of ice jolted its way out of the bucket, shattering the rock somewhere between the two men.

The Professor stopped his charge. Now, out of stored power and ideas, there was nothing more he could say or do.

A moment of silence ensued. Kaustos then spoke,

"I can only imagine your confusion and disappointment."

Shiloh Callaghan

At a time like this, *YOU* may expect Kaustos to give some drawn out monologue or a tell-all confession of all his wise ways of trickery and deceit. But that was never his formula. Like Solemn, The Professor had served his purpose. And now, while Kaustos enemy is weak, this is the time to go in for the kill.

He picked up the bucket of water and without hesitation threw the rest in the air. Stone could do nothing as he watched death approach. Now injected with power, the water began molding from a shapeless loose puddle into the shape of a long blade of ice.

"I'm sorry!" Yelled The Professor, hoping the kids would hear him.

With the force of a cannon, it finally crashed into his heart.

Stones eyes gazed downward as he dropped to his knee's.

"My shirt... is covered...covered in...water?!"

Not only was that the confused thought of The Professor but also of Kaustos (changing the "my" to "his" of course... and adding a few expletives)

"Impossible!" Yelled Kaustos. Quickly he power-grabbed the first stone that The Professor threw and flung it at his enemy.

SMACK!

Paradise Lost

168

"I hardly felt that!" exclaimed The Professor with a slight bloody nose.

Kaustos was beside himself. It was as if all the natural elements had lost their innate power. Completely enraged, Kaustos lost focus, and although only for a second, he let down his defenses.

CLICK!

Professor: "Well, that was easier than I thought."

Kaustos looked down at the shackles molesting* his hands. He felt that familiar feeling of disgust in his mouth as he breathed through a rusty old filter. This still is what he wanted. But how it happened, that was a new mystery.

"How? How on earth did you get the elements to loose their power?!" he asked, with hunger in his voice.

"I didn't. Maybe *IT* did." answered The Professor looking toward YOU.

"Preposterous!"

"If not *IT*, than The Tower. Either way, Someone of great power wants you to lose. NOW MOVE!"

*(that's definition 2 of the word molesting, they weren't actually sexually assaulting his hands.)

Shiloh Callaghan

ACT6 SCENE13: Collin

You may remember at the beginning of all this, he was quite the focal point. Slowly and progressively, however; he faded into the group, becoming not a lead role but just another character. However the scene of this story is changing yet again. *YOU* see, despite the reason, he is a murderer, a heart stained in the blood of another. And in this world, for good or bad, that will make him special.

Look! Someone is getting ready to speak.

Philip: "So what now, those shackles won't last forever."

He, Collin, The professor and even the tigers all stood on one side of Kaustos, glaring at him with disgust. Willow would also have been glaring, if she wasn't still passed out.

"That is true." replied Stone "I'm already storing power for new ones. But the details of the future don't concern me as much as those of the past."

He approached Kaustos, "Why do all of this, Kaustos, just to be trapped again?"

The Villain grinned, "Expecting an answer with nothing in return is called a favor. Do you really expect me to do a favor for a 'creator of love', that would just make me feel CLEAN!" he replied with distain. "But for a fellow killer like me, I might give an answer."
"Don't be preposterous, there are no killers here!" assured The Professor.

Paradise Lost

"AH! So you didn't see! I was curious why the boy was still in your good graces."

"What is he talking about!?" asked Stone, looking at Collin and Philip. Neither of which spoke up.

"Oh come on!" yelled Kaustos toward Collin "You blew a hole in my best mate and no amount of shame will pardon THAT particular sin, so you might as well relish in it, boy!"

"I'm not you!" fired back Collin with tears trolling from his eyes.

Kaustos: "Not yet!"

"Collin!" interrupted The Professor "What is he babbling about!?"

He wanted to reply, but words failed him.

"It cant be true!?" Spoke The Professor in disbelief.

Philip now stepped forward. "The Mayor wasn't dead, the prophecy lied to you, Professor. He was going to kill me, Collin saved my life!"

Kaustos: "Why not shoot his hands boy?! Why shoot him in the heart!? You wanted to KILL didn't you!?"

"NO! It all happened so fast... I just reacted!"

"You didn't react, you murdered! And that's eternal imprisonment, those are the rules, Stone and you know it!"

Shiloh Callaghan

Kaustos snapped his eyes back to Collin, "Looks like I will have a bunk mate. Until death do us part boy!"

The Professor quickly gagged Kaustos mouth with a small turtle shell inside his mask (i know, weird right?) to keep him quiet.

"No more of your poisonous words!" He demanded.

Staring back at Collin with all sternness, The Professor continued "Kaustos is right, you know? Those are the rules."

"I know" replied Collin with tearful eyes.

"But he saved my life!" Yelled Philip "Why should he..."

"Quite!" demanded Stone. "Let me finish." Looking again at Collin he continued, "And if you were born of my generation, I would certainly have to enforce that rule."

Collin raised his head with a glimmer of hope.

"However you weren't raised in a paradise, you never knew perfection. So I don't believe you should be held to the same moral standard." The Professor approached Collin and put his arm around him, "It's okay, son. I just hope the pain you feel now will guide you to better choices in the future."

He felt comforted, not at all clean.

Stone removed the turtle shell from Kaustos mouth.

Paradise Lost

The Professor: "No boy bunks with you, freak!"

"Surely that wasn't my intention!"

"So what is? What is your intention for all of this?"

"As I said before, I don't do favors for the likes of you. But I will make a demand which will benefit us both. Take to me The Mayor, I want to see his body. Do that, and I will tell you what you need to know. "

"What? It's just that simple?" asked The Professor with a complete lack of trust.

Kaustos nodded.

"For what possible purpose?"

"Let's just say, people have all sorts of fetishes. Mine are just of a more morbid nature."

"You are a corpse-pervert!?" Spoke Philip, wanting to vomit.

The Villain smiled a sick smile.

Kaustos is, without a doubt, a freak. Even The Tigers cringed at his proposal. However twisted as he was, though, The Professor knew his stubbornness. These were his terms, a one time deal never to be repeated again. Like the man said, it was a demand.

The Professor: "How do we know you aren't going to lie?"

Shiloh Callaghan

"Even if I do, what do you have to loose?"

"He is right." spoke up Collin. "Let's go and see the body."

<u>ACT6 SCENE14: The finale</u>

THUMP! Went Willow's fist into Philips chubby arm.

"I'm sorry!" He apologized "It was reasonable to believe you would be awakened by a kiss! You should be happy... you never had it so good!"

CRACK! This time the violence hit his chest.

"That wasn't reasonable thinking, Philip" interjected The Professor. "It's obvious that one of us had to give her some of our energy to awaken her. A kiss is just silly."

Rubbing his man-boob, he replied, "You didn't have to tell her."

"No crying over spilled milk, young man."

Shortly they all reached the world's end.

Looking over in the distance, there was the body, slumped sideways by the tree with a dagger still in hand.

Collin started to walk over until The Professor grabbed him by his shoulder.

Collin: "It's okay, I'll go with Kaustos." He replied "I **need** to see what I did, I **want** to feel the pain."

The Professor thought for a second, then let him go.
"Collin!" shouted Philip

Shiloh Callaghan

"Yes?"

"If Kaustos tries anything, I'll power-push him off the cliff!"

SMACK! This time it was The Professors hand hitting Philip upside his head. "No one will repay violence with violence! And there is no sense in going alone with Kaustos. We will go together. Seeing the body will serve as a warning for us all."

"Can we hurry up, my date is waiting!" spoke Kaustos freakishly.

"The Tigers will go first!" instructed The Professor.

They all waited a minute for the two cats to sniff and look around the body for any booby traps.

"Clever" noticed Kaustos, "I should have thought about that!"

2 deep grunts signaled that all was okay.

As Kaustos began to walk forward, Philip asked him, "Should we close our eyes or something? I want to keep chaste."

The evil one gave no response as he approached the body. Standing in-between Solemn and the edge of the world, Kaustos kicked the body over onto its back. The others closed in to take a look.

Paradise Lost

Seeing the gaping hole in his chest made them all feel sick. Kaustos bent down and put his ear to The Mayors mouth.

"He IS dead."

"Obviously!" replied Willow.

Kaustos: "Yes, but dead dead! Nothing can bring him back." He closed his eyes with a deep and perverse feeling of satisfaction, "What a wonderful realization!"

"How much longer, Kaustos?" asked Stone with disgust.

 Backing away from the body he pointed to Solemn's right-side pant pocket.

"Your answer lies on a piece of paper" He said.

They all huddled in as Kaustos, although still in eye-sight, slipped back.

The Professor dug into the pocket and pulled out the piece of paper.

"Unfold it" directed Kaustos.

It took four motions to open the paper, with each one building more anticipation than the previous.

As The Professor finally opened it, all eyes, including *YOURS* were captive to the answer it held.

WHOOSH!

Shiloh Callaghan

Collin: "It's the Tower?"

"Kaustos, what is this?" asked The Professor "...Kaustos?"

Everyone quickly turned back.

"He jumped!" yelled Collin as he ran to the edge.

Looking down into the clouds below, *YOU* could see the imprint of Kaustos big body slowly fading away into its haze.

Collin and Willow looked at Philip.

Philip: "What? Don't look at me, I didn't push him! It's a bit anticlimactic though, him just jumping over the edge like that."

Collin: "Why would he jump? Professor?"

"The symbols...they are different."

"What?"

"The symbols on The Tower, they are different."

"Professor, Kaustos just offed himself, what does the picture have to do with that?"

"Everything" he replied seriously. "Let's go to The Tower."

Paradise Lost

ACT6 SCENE15: Prophecy of fiction

Willow looked at the picture, comparing it with The Tower now in front of them, "It looks exactly the same Professor, there isn't any difference."

"That's the point!"

"What point?"

"Watch and see my child."

Standing a safe distance away, Stone sent a blast of energy toward The Tower.

BOOM!

Upon impact, the exterior immediately began to crack and give way. Falling off like old plaster, the imitation surface began crumbling to the ground.

"Ah ha!"

The Professor began stomping around like a little girl in a temper tantrum,

"That clever-evil old, dead, disgusting, fart-faced despicable fiend! He created a veneer! I was too excited, too rushed to notice last time, the real prophecy is underneath!"

Shiloh Callaghan

"So everything you saw and told us about was from Kaustos?" asked Collin. (The Professor nodded) "But why would he kills himself?"

"That's what I intend to find out! *YOU*!" shouted The Professor, "Don't be shy, come over here and let's take a look!

Go over and look (continue reading)

Don't go over and look (please go to The Table of Possible Context)

"OH GROSS!!!" screamed the kids as The Professor linked into your eyes. A few peaceful seconds of silence went by before the children would hear random outburst of almost-curse-words flying out of Stones mouth. For example things like, "Farfegnugen!" and "Butter balds!" "CAAAACKOOO!" It became so annoying even the tigers began to cover their ears. And as the seconds turned to minutes, which then turned to hours (2 to be precise) The once excited children, slowly and painfully began to loose interest..."KLABAGABL!"

Finally, The Professor detached himself from you and was ready to tell what he saw. However as he looked back, he noticed an audience which had all went to sleep, all that is but Collin.

"They got tired of waiting?" he spoke with a soft smile.

"But not you?"

Paradise Lost

"No" he replied, still with regret in his breath. "So, what did it say?"

"In all the possible future scenarios, there was ever only one end for Kaustos."

"Which was?"

"Death."

"But, how could that be? If he was the only one that knew the future, couldn't he change it anyway he desired?"

"If our world was as simple as you and me Collin, he could have. But like I have been trying to teach you, not seeing doesn't always mean we don't believe. Whoever made The Tower, isn't evil." The Professor smiled. "The likes of Kaustos will never inherit this world."

Collin thought for a second as he soaked in The Professors words. "But is he good?"

"If we view justice through his eyes." replied The Professor (admittedly with a slight lack of confidence.) "Collin, there was a reason Kaustos chose this particular death, the one where we are still alive."

"Why? What does The Tower say?"

"I think you should see for yourself."

Stone pointed Collin toward the symbols that lay on the underbelly of The Floating Tower.

Shiloh Callaghan

The Professor: "Will *YOU* please join him?"

Yes (keep reading)

No (please go to The Table of Possible Context)

Are *YOU* ready? For here lies the answer to the entire story. Go ahead, connect with the boy and as if reading a book flip the page. There is where the answer lies.

Paradise Lost

Only through one who has taken a life, will all fallen life breathe again. However let truth be told, only at the cost of the one life, that is his own.

Do you accept?

Shiloh Callaghan

What evil person would give up his life to save those of his victims? No, not even a bad man, let alone an evil one. But a good man? He would.

But then again in this world a good man wouldn't have a victim's blood on his hands in the first place.

Ah! But an innocent yet foolish boy? One Tempered and trained by a good man but still capable of evil works...He would do. He would give his life for all that have fallen, even if one of them was pure evil.

The real prophecy had ended with the death of Kaustos. The future is not yet written. But when it is, YOU are invited to come back. Come and observe, watch the final outcome of the story YOU YOURSELF have helped write.

To be continued...

Paradise Lost

Table of possible context

Page 24
YOU died. The End

Page 45
Straight ahead is the prison door! Hurry you are almost there.

Kaustos voice is echoing through the hallway, can YOU hear him?
They are behind you! Don't worry about opening the door, just pass through it.
Now what?! Where are YOU going to go?

Look around, what do YOU see? What's ...

Kaustos: "Good! (They touched YOU). IT's just as scared of us as we are of IT Collin. Wipe that worry off of your face, you only touched IT, you didn't hurt IT.

Collin: "Your hands! You are free!"

Kaustos: "You are too Collin, or at least you will think you are when you awaken."

Collin: "What? I..."

With one swift movement of Kaustos finger, the boy collapsed to the ground.

Shiloh Callaghan

Kaustos: "YOU tried to run? Honestly where are YOU going to go? This is my world, not YOURS!"
(Please return to the story)

Page 80
Professor Stone: "Oh! I get it... YOU are attracted to me and YOU feel a little nervous with me so near. It's okay, don't feel in anyway embarrassed. Admittedly I have this effect on most living things. I once had a rather fetching Cherry Blossom Tree for a suitor, long story. I am flattered, but how can I say this.... Not interested. I prefer a beautiful visible woman, I'm afraid this will never work.

Now that that uncomfortableness is out of the way, let's return to the matter at hand."
(Please return to the story)

Page 104
Willow: "I figured that much, binocular face!"
(Please return to the story)

Page 105
Willow: "I hope you get bitten by a Hepatitis-monkey!"

Page 121
The Professor (whispering): "Personally, I find it best to deal with rejection gracefully. Just because I refused your advances before is no reason to make a spectacle in front of

Paradise Lost

the children. Now I am going to back away and pretend this conversation never happened."

(Please return to the story)

Page 155
Kaustos: "YOU're as stubborn as I am. It's a respectable quality. However, in this case it enhances one of YOUR more outstanding characteristics, cowardice. Afraid of what may happen if YOU obey my words? YOU should be. Now listen carefully, because...
(Please return to the story)

Page 163
Zoom out a little more... A little more. Good!
(Please return to the story)

Page 179
YOU died. The End

Page 181
YOU poop in YOUR pants then YOU die. The End

Shiloh Callaghan

ACT6 SCENE16: The beginning of The End

The Professor: Did you see it, son?"

Collin: "Yes"

The Professor: "And what is your decision?"

Collin: "The right one."

The Professor: "I'm sorry... it just, doesn't seem fair"

Collin: (no response)

The Professor: "So what now?"

Collin: "Shovels, we each need one."

The Professor: "For what?"

Collin: "To dig up graves, all of them. We should get started soon, this may take a while."

Paradise Lost

About the author

Shiloh Callaghan was born in the Areop'agus of our age, Berkeley California.

For the past decade, throughout the earth he has been a teacher, writer, public speaker and skateboarder who has striven to bring meaning to people's lives through his work (and his skateboarding).

Behind every story, there are real life adventures that he has either experienced somewhere in the world, or he has seen firsthand.

Shiloh Callaghan

From living with tribesmen, to dinning with future kings, Shiloh has led a life rich with... Well, life!

"I am not a Rhodes Scholar, I am a Rogue scholar," he says jokingly. This idea keeps him on an ever-moving quest throughout the globe, in hopes to enrich not only his life but to also enrich yours.

Contact Me:
shiloh@cipherbooks.com
(Discover other titles by Shiloh Callaghan at
cipherbooks.com)

Paradise Lost